"Why Don't You Take A Few Days To Make Your Decision?" Christian Offered.

"According to the will, you've got a couple of weeks to take your place at the resort." He scribbled his cell number on the back of his business card, then handed it to her.

She ran her thumb over the embossed lettering in a slow stroke that was mesmerizing to Christian. His body stirred and he shifted uncomfortably on his chair.

What he'd like to do was blow off the business talk, take her for an elegant meal and then off to his hotel. If she was any other woman, that's exactly what he would do.

But Erica Prentice was off-limits. If she ended up going to Aspen, his body had better get used to living with disappointment.

"We both know what that decision will be."

"You're going to accept the conditions of the will?"

"How can I not?"

Dear Reader,

It's always exciting being invited to take part in a continuity series for Silhouette Desire. First, because I *love* writing Desires. Second, because it gives me a chance to work closely with some of the amazing writers in the line.

This time was no exception. In the Jarrod continuity, my book is first. I get the chance to introduce characters, and show you the location of our stories. If I've done my job right, then hopefully you'll be convinced to stick around and read the next five books in this series.

The Jarrod dynasty was born in Aspen, Colorado, more than a hundred years ago. The family's grown along with the town and now the Jarrod Resort is the epitome of lush extravagance. The Jarrod family itself is what all Desire families should be—larger than life. In this series, there are secrets to uncover, hidden loves to reveal and happy endings to find.

In my book, you'll meet Christian Hanford, an attorney who owes everything to the late Donald Jarrod. And his heroine is Erica Prentice, a woman whose life is about to be turned upside down.

I hope you'll enjoy yourselves with this first installment of Dynasties: The Jarrods. And I hope you'll let us all know what you think! E-mail me at maureenchildbooks@gmail.com or snail mail me at P.O. Box 1883, Westminster, CA 92684-1883.

And happy reading!

Maureen

MAUREEN CHILD

CLAIMING HER BILLION-DOLLAR BIRTHRIGHT

Published by Silhouette Books
America's Publisher of Contemporary Romance

Special thanks and acknowledgment to Maureen Child for her contribution to the Dynasties: The Jarrods miniseries.

To family.
Mine. Yours.
And to all the wonderful, irritating moments
we share with them.

SILHOUETTE BOOKS

Recycling programs
for this product may
not exist in your area.

ISBN-13: 978-0-373-73037-7

CLAIMING HER BILLION-DOLLAR BIRTHRIGHT

Copyright © 2010 by Harlequin Books S.A.

Visit Silhouette Books at www.eHarlequin.com

Printed in U.S.A.

Books by Maureen Child

Silhouette Desire

The Part-Time Wife #1755
Beyond the Boardroom #1765
Thirty Day Affair #1785
†*Scorned by the Boss* #1816
†*Seduced by the Rich Man* #1820
†*Captured by the Billionaire* #1826
††*Bargaining for King's Baby* #1857
††*Marrying for King's Millions* #1862
††*Falling for King's Fortune* #1868
High-Society Secret Pregnancy #1879
Baby Bonanza #1893
An Officer and a Millionaire #1915
Seduced Into a Paper Marriage #1946
††*Conquering King's Heart* #1965
††*Claiming King's Baby* #1971
††*Wedding at King's Convenience* #1978
††*The Last Lone Wolf* #2011
Claiming Her Billion-Dollar Birthright #2024

†Reasons for Revenge
††Kings of California

MAUREEN CHILD

is a California native who loves to travel. Every chance they get, she and her husband are taking off on another research trip. The author of more than sixty books, Maureen loves a happy ending and still swears that she has the best job in the world. She lives in Southern California with her husband, two children and a golden retriever with delusions of grandeur. Visit Maureen's Web site at www.maureenchild.com.

From The Last Will And Testament Of Donald Jarrod

…and to my youngest child, my daughter **Erica Prentice,** I bequeath the sixth portion of my estate. Erica, I understand that your inclusion in this document will be a surprise to not only yourself, but to your brothers and sister, as well. It is my deepest wish that you will find a way to become part of the Jarrod family, fractured though it is. I am also leaving you the theater program for the play where I was first so lucky to have met your mother. I've kept this tattered playbill as a remembrance of your lovely mother…as a remembrance of you. It is my hope that, by giving you a place at Jarrod Ridge, I've also given you a chance to know some part of me, as well.

Prologue

Christian Hanford refused to sit in a dead man's chair.

So instead, he walked to the front of Don Jarrod's desk and perched uneasily on the edge. The old man's study was in the family living quarters on the top floor of Jarrod Manor. Here at Jarrod Ridge resort, everything was luxurious. Even a study that the public never saw. Paneled walls, thick carpets, original oils on the walls and a massive fireplace built of river stones. Of course, there was no cheerful blaze in the hearth, since summer had settled over Colorado.

He imagined none of the people in the room felt cheerful anyway. How could he blame them? They'd lost their father only a week before and now, they'd just had the proverbial rug pulled out from under them.

Years ago, each of the Jarrod children had left Jarrod Ridge, the plush resort that had been in their family for generations, to make their own way. Their father had pushed them all so hard to succeed that he'd managed to drive them away, one by one. To come back now, when it was too late to mend fences, was a hard thing to accept.

Not to mention the fact that in death, Don had figured out a way to not only bring them all home—but to keep them there. Something he hadn't been able to do in life.

The huge Jarrod estate was to be divided equally among his children—on the condition that they all move home and take over running their legacy. Each of the Jarrod siblings had been slapped hard and none of them were happy about it. The old man had found a way to control them from the grave.

Which wasn't sitting well.

Christian watched them all, understanding how they must feel, but sworn to abide by his late client's wishes. God knows he'd tried to talk Don out of this, but the old man had been nothing if not stubborn.

Blake Jarrod and his brother Guy were the oldest. Though not identical, the twins each carried the stamp of their father. Blake was more the buttoned-down type, while Guy was a bit more easygoing. Gavin was two years younger than the twins, but he and Blake had worked together for quite a while out in Vegas.

Trevor Jarrod was the most laid-back of the bunch—or at least that was the demeanor he showed the world. Then there was Melissa. The youngest and the only girl.

Or so she thought.

Christian sent a mental kick out to his now deceased mentor for leaving him in this position. But even in death, Don had wanted to rule the Jarrod clan and no doubt, wherever he was now, he didn't really care that it was Christian getting stuck with the dirty work.

Blake stood up as if he couldn't bear sitting still another minute. Just a week since Don Jarrod's death, none of his children had had a chance to come to terms with his passing. And now they'd all been sucker punched.

They'd left the cemetery just an hour before and after reading through most of the will's bequests, emotions were running high. Well, Christian thought, they were about to go even higher.

"Why are we still here, Christian?" Guy asked from his seat, bracing his elbows on his knees. "You've read the will, what's left to say?"

"There's one more thing to cover."

"What haven't you covered?" Trevor asked, shifting a glance around the room at his brothers and sister. "Seems pretty clear to me. Dad's arranged things to get us back to Jarrod Ridge. Just like he always wanted."

"I still can't believe he's gone," Melissa whispered.

Gavin dropped one arm around her shoulders and gave her a supportive hug. "It'll be okay, Mel."

"Will it?" Blake asked. "We've all got lives separate from the Ridge. Now we're supposed to walk away from whatever we've built to come back home and take over?"

"I understand how you feel," Christian said softly and waited until all eyes were on him. "I do. I told Don this wasn't the way to handle things."

"Let me guess," Guy interrupted, "Dad wouldn't listen."

"He had his own ideas."

"Always did," Trevor mused.

"The point is," Blake said, voice loud enough that everyone settled down to hear him, "Dad split the estate up equally between the five of us. So what's left to talk about?"

There was his opening, Christian thought, bracing himself for what would come in response to his next statement. "The fact that the estate's been split, not into five equal shares, but *six*."

"Six?" Gavin repeated, glancing around at his siblings as if doing an unnecessary head count. "But there are only five of us."

"Don's last surprise," Christian said quietly. "You have a sister you've never met."

made her wary even as her hormones continued to do a dance of appreciation.

Erica waved him to one of the two chairs opposite her desk. "I have to admit, I'm intrigued. Why would a lawyer from Colorado come all this way to see me?"

"It's a long story," he said, glancing around her office.

She knew what he was seeing and that he was probably singularly unimpressed. The beige walls of the tiny room were mostly bare but for two paintings she'd brought from home to lessen the grim atmosphere. Erica's office was nearly claustrophobic, as befitting someone just getting started on their career. Of course, she thought, not for the first time, if she'd been offered a job in the family company, things would have been different.

Though her older brothers all ran different arms of the Prentice Group, Erica's father had made it clear that she wouldn't be a part of the family business. They'd never been close, she thought, but she'd hoped that she'd be given at least a chance to prove herself, as her brothers had. But her father wasn't a man you could argue with and once his mind was made up, the decision might as well have been set in concrete.

Still, she thought, dragging her brain away from the problems of family, now wasn't the time to be thinking about any of that. As tempting as it might be to indulge in a long meeting with a gorgeous lawyer watching her through amazingly dark chocolate eyes, she simply didn't have time for it today. As it was, she'd only managed to squeeze out a few minutes from her already packed schedule to accommodate Christian Hanford. She couldn't give him more.

Leaning forward, she folded her hands on her desktop and smiled. "I'm sorry, but your long story will have to wait for another time. I have another appointment in fifteen minutes, Mr. Hanford, so if you wouldn't mind, could you just tell me what you're doing here?"

His gaze met hers and held. Erica couldn't have looked away if she had wanted to.

"I represent the estate of Donald Jarrod," he said quietly.

"Jarrod." Erica thought about the name, trying to place it, when suddenly, she made the connection. "Colorado. Jarrod. You mean the Jarrod resort in Aspen, Jarrod?"

He gave her a brief smile and inclined his head. Reaching down for the briefcase at his feet, he pulled it onto his lap, opened it and took out a legal-size, manila envelope. Sliding it across the desk to her, he said, "Yes, *that* Donald Jarrod."

Confused but curious, Erica picked up the envelope and opened it. She pulled out a document and glanced at the title. "His *will?* Why do I have a copy of the man's will?"

"Because, Ms. Prentice, you're one of the beneficiaries."

She glanced from the document to him and back again. Her stomach did a wild spin and flutter that left her feeling off balance.

"That makes no sense," she murmured, slipping the will back into the envelope and deliberately flattening the brass clasp. "I've never met the man. Why would he leave me anything in his will?"

His features tightened and Erica thought she caught a glimpse of sympathy shining in his eyes before he took the envelope back from her and slid it into his briefcase. "I told you it was going to be a long story."

"Right." She watched him close up his black leather case and wished she had the document in her hands again. She'd like the chance to read it herself before they went any further. But apparently, Christian Hanford wanted his say first. Which didn't do a thing to ease the tension flooding her system.

What was happening here? How had her average, run-of-the-mill day taken such a bizarre turn? And what did a dead empire builder from Colorado have to do with her?

"Then perhaps we can meet later, when you have more time."

She didn't want to wait, but didn't see how she could avoid it.

"Time. Yes. That's probably a good idea. I'm…" Erica shook her head, met his gaze and said, "I'm sorry. This is just all so confusing. Maybe if you gave me some idea what this was about. Why I was mentioned in his will…"

"I think it's best to get this done all at once," he said. "No point in getting into it now when we can't finish it."

He stood up and Erica was forced to tip her head back to look up at him. That frisson of attraction was still there, but now there was more. There was a sense that once she met with Christian Hanford and heard the whole story, nothing in her life was ever going to be the same.

She could see the truth in his eyes. He was watching her as if he could read her mind and knew exactly what a tumult her thoughts were in. She read understanding in his eyes and once again thought she caught a flicker of sympathy.

Nerves rattled through her and Erica knew she'd never make it through her whole day now without knowing what was going on. How could she possibly meet with clients and do the myriad other little jobs that required her attention with this mystery hanging over her head?

Nope, an impossible task. On impulse, she stood up and said, "On second thought, I think we should have that talk now. If you could give me a half an hour to clear up a few things, we could meet..."

Where? Not her apartment. She wasn't inviting a strange man into her home, even if he was a lawyer. Not here in the office. If she was about to get hit with bad news, she'd rather it wasn't done in front of people she had to work with every day.

As if he were still reading scatter-shot thoughts, Christian offered, "Why don't we meet for lunch? I'll come back in an hour and then we'll talk."

She nodded. "One hour."

Once he'd left, Erica took a deep breath in a futile attempt to steady herself. Her stomach was jumping with nerves and her mind was whirling. What in the world was going on? Once again, she was tempted to call her father and ask his advice. But at the same time, she knew he would simply tell her to think it through and make her own decisions. Walter Prentice had never been the kind of man to "mollycoddle" his children. Not even his youngest child and only daughter.

No, she would meet with Christian Hanford, get to the bottom of this and then decide what to do about it.

But before she could do that, she had to clear her appointments for the day. She had no idea how long this meeting with Christian Hanford was going to take—or if she'd be in any kind of mood to deal with business once their meeting was over. She hit a button on her phone. Her assistant, Monica, opened the office door an instant later. Her blue eyes sparkling, she asked, "What's up with Mr. Gorgeous?"

Erica sighed. Monica was more friend than assistant. They'd bonded shortly after Erica had come to work for B&B nearly a year ago. The two of them were the youngest employees in the company and they'd forged a friendly working relationship that had resulted in lots of after-business drinks and dinners. But today, Erica was feeling too jumbled to enjoy her friend's teasing.

"I have no idea."

Monica's smile faded. "Hey, are you okay?"

"I'll let you know later," she said, sitting down at her desk again. "For now, I need you to cancel today's meetings. I've got something important to take care of."

"That won't be difficult. When do you want everything rescheduled?"

"Work everyone in as quickly as possible," Erica told her. "We'll just double up a little and stay late if we have to."

"Okay," Monica said. "This does sound important. Is everything all right?"

"Honestly, I don't know." The unsettled feeling in the pit of her stomach kept warning her that things were about to get very weird.

And there wasn't a thing she could do to avoid it.

Christian was waiting for her when Erica came down the elevator and crossed the lobby of the office building. Something inside him stirred at the sight of her. He'd felt it earlier, too. The moment he'd looked into her whiskey-brown eyes, Christian had known that this woman was going to be trouble.

He didn't do trouble. Not for years, now. He had exactly what he'd spent most of his life working toward. A position of respect and more money than he could spend in two lifetimes. He hadn't worked his ass off for years to get where he was just to let it all go because his body had reacted to the wrong woman.

And Erica Prentice was definitely off-limits to him.

Not only was she the illegitimate daughter of his long-time employer…there was also the fact that any "fraternization" with members of the Jarrod family could see him lose the job he valued so much.

Hadn't ever been an issue for him before this. Melissa Jarrod was a sweetheart, but she'd never interested him.

But he had the distinct feeling that Erica Prentice was going to be a different matter altogether.

As she crossed the glossy floor, his gaze took in everything about her. Shoulder-length light brown hair, soft and touchable. Smooth, pale skin, amber eyes and a mouth that had a tendency to quirk to one side as if she were trying to decide whether to smile or not. She was short, but curvy, the kind of woman that made a man want to sweep her up and pull her in close. Not that he had any intention of doing anything like that.

Her eyes met his and Christian told himself to take care of business and get back to the jet waiting for him at the airport. Safer all around if he concluded this trip as quickly as possible.

"Sorry I'm late," she said as she joined him.

"No problem." Of course the fact that he wanted to take her hand again just for an excuse to touch her might be looked on as a problem. Shaking his head to dislodge that thought, he said, "Look, I saw a café just down the street. Why don't we go have some lunch and get this situation taken care of?"

"Fine." She headed for the glass doors and walked outside when they swished open automatically. She stopped on the sidewalk and pushed her hair out of her eyes when a cold San Francisco wind tossed it into the air. Looking up at him, she asked, "Tell me this much first. Are you about to make me happy? Or is this going to screw up my world?"

Christian looked down into eyes shining with trepidation. "To tell the truth, maybe a little of both."

Two

"You must be crazy," Erica said fifteen minutes later.

The outdoor Italian café sat at the corner of a busy intersection in downtown San Francisco. Only a few of the dozen small round tables covered in bloodred tablecloths were occupied by people stopping for an early lunch. Inside the restaurant there were less hardy souls, diners not wanting to deal with the capricious wind. Fabrizio's was one of Erica's favorite places, but now she was sure this visit was going to forever take the shine off the restaurant for her.

Staring across the table at the man who watched her through steady eyes, she repeated what she'd said only moments before. "You're wrong. This is crazy. I am *not* Donald Jarrod's illegitimate heir."

Their waiter came up to the table just as she finished speaking and Erica felt heat rush up her neck and fill her cheeks. She only hoped the man hadn't heard her. That would be perfect. She was known here. People would talk. Speculate.

They would anyway, she realized. The Jarrod family, much like the Prentice family, was big news. Even if this wasn't true—which, she assured herself silently, it wasn't—word would get out and soon Erica would be the subject of tabloid gossip and whispered innuendos from those she knew.

She could just imagine the reactions from her father and stepmother, Angela. Walter Prentice loathed scandal. He'd raised his children to believe that family business was private and that getting one's name in the paper was not something to be desired. Now, Erica thought, ancient dirty laundry would be spread out for the world to read about and enjoy and she and her family would be the punch line to mean-spirited jokes told at cocktail parties.

Oh, God, this just couldn't be happening.

"Iced tea for the lady," the waiter was saying as he divested his tray of drinks, "and coffee for the gentleman. Have you decided on lunch?"

"No," Christian said. "We need a few minutes."

"Take your time," the young man told him, then gave them each a smile and left them alone with their menus.

Erica didn't even glance at hers. She wasn't sure she'd ever be hungry again. She grabbed her tea, took a long drink to ease the dryness in her throat and then set the glass down. Keeping her voice low enough that Christian was forced to lean across the table to hear her over the discordant hum of traffic, she said, "I don't know what this is about, or what you're up to, but…"

"If you'll hear me out, I'll try to explain."

He looked as if he wished he were anywhere but there and Erica knew exactly how he felt. She wanted nothing more than to jump up, vault over the iron railing separating the café tables from the sidewalk and disappear into the crowds. But since that wasn't going to happen, she told herself to remain calm and listen to him. Once he was finished saying his piece, she'd simply walk away and put this hideous conversation out of her mind forever.

He threw a quick glance at the table closest to them as if to assure himself he wouldn't be overheard, then he looked back to Erica. His dark chocolate eyes shone with determination as he said quietly, "I realize this is a shock—"

"It would be if it were true," she allowed.

"It is true, Ms. Prentice." His voice dropped another notch. "Would I be here if this were all some elaborate joke?"

"Maybe," she said. "For all I know this is some sort of extortion attempt or something."

Now those dark eyes of his fired with indignation. "I'm an attorney. I'm here at the behest of my late employer. It was his final wish that I come to you personally to deliver this news."

Erica nodded, seeing the insult her jibe had delivered and said, "Fine. It's not a joke. But it *is* a mistake.

Believe me when I tell you, I'm the daughter of Walter Prentice."

"No," he said tightly. "You're not. I have documentation to back me up."

She took a breath of the cold, clear air, hoping it would brace her for what was coming. If this was a mistake, she'd find out soon enough. If it was all true, she needed to see proof. "Show me."

He delved into his briefcase and handed her a smaller manila envelope than the one he'd shown her earlier at her office. Warily, she took it, her fingers barely touching it, as if she half expected the thing to blow up in her hands. But it didn't and she opened the clasp and slid free the three sheets of paper inside.

The first document was a letter. Written to Don Jarrod and signed by…Erica's mother. Her heart lodged in her throat as she stared at the elegant handwriting. Her mother had died in childbirth, so Erica had always felt cheated out of a relationship with the woman her brothers remembered so clearly. Danielle Prentice had kept a journal though, one that had been passed on to Erica when she was sixteen. She'd spent hours reading those pages, getting to know the mother she'd never known. So she recognized that beautiful, familiar handwriting and it was almost as if her mother were there with them at the table.

The note was brief, but Erica felt the grief in the words written there.

My dear Don,
I wanted you to know that I don't regret our time

together. Though what we shared was never meant to last, I will always remember you with affection. That said, you must see that you can never acknowledge our child. Walter has forgiven me and has promised to love this child as he has our sons. And so I ask that you stay away and let us rebuild our lives. It's best for all of us.

Love,

Danielle

Shock faded into stunned, reluctant acceptance as Erica's eyes misted over with tears. Not once in her journals had Danielle ever even hinted at the affair she had had with Don Jarrod. Yet these few, simple words were impossible to deny even as the page before her blurred and she blinked frantically to clear her vision. Slowly she traced the tip of one finger across the faded ink, as if she could actually touch her mother. Though a ball of ice had settled in the pit of her stomach, she realized that this letter explained so much.

Walter had never been an overly affectionate father, even with Erica's older brothers. But with her, Walter had been even more…distant. Now at least, she knew why. She wasn't his child. She was, instead, a constant reminder of his wife's infidelity. Oh, God.

Christian was sitting there across from her and not speaking, and for that she was grateful. If he tried to say something kind or sweet or sympathetic, she'd lose what little control she was desperately clinging to.

She lifted her gaze to look at him and said in a last-ditch attempt to avoid the inevitable, "How do I know my mother actually wrote this letter? For all I know you've had it forged for your own reasons."

"And what could those be?" Christian asked. "What possible reason could the Jarrod family have for lying about this?"

"I don't know," she admitted as she frantically tried to come up with something, anything that might explain all of this away. Her family wasn't a close one, but they were all she had. If she accepted this as truth, wouldn't that mean she would lose them all?

"Look at the other two papers," he urged, taking a sip of his coffee.

She didn't want to, but didn't know how to avoid it. Pretending this day had never happened, that Christian Hanford had never appeared at her office, wouldn't work. Hiding her head in the sand wouldn't change anything. If this were actually true, then she had to know. And if it were all some elaborate lie, then she had to know that, too.

Nodding to herself, she looked at the next paper and froze in place. It was a letter from her father to Donald Jarrod and it managed, in a few short lines, to completely disintegrate the last of her doubts.

Jarrod,
My wife is dead, delivering your daughter. This letter is as close as you'll ever get to the child, make no mistake. If you try to get around me, I'll see to it that you regret it.
Walter Prentice

"Oh, my God." Erica slumped against her chair and looked at Christian.

"I'm sorry this is so hard." His voice was without inflection, but she thought she caught the sheen of sincerity in his dark brown eyes. Still, his being sorry didn't change anything.

"I don't even know what to say," she whispered, staring at her father's handwriting. She'd have known that scrawl anywhere. She knew it was genuine because as her older brothers had long said, what forger could ever reproduce such hideous writing?

God. Her brothers.

Half brothers.

Did they all know? Had they been lying to her, too, all these years? Was nothing in her life what she'd thought it was? If she wasn't Erica Prentice, then just who was she?

"Ms. Prentice...Erica," Christian said, "I know you're having a hard time with this."

"I don't think you could have the slightest idea," she told him.

"Fair enough," he said. "But I do know that your biological father regretted never being able to know you."

"Did he?" She shook her head, unsure just what she felt about Donald Jarrod. What kind of man was it who slept with another man's wife? Who created a child and then never made an attempt to acknowledge it? Had Walter's letter really kept Don Jarrod away? Was he that easily put off? Had his affair with Danielle and Erica's birth meant nothing to him?

As if he knew exactly where her thoughts had taken her, Christian said, "Donald's wife, Margaret, died of cancer, leaving him with five children to raise alone when the youngest, your sister Melissa, was only two."

"My sister," she repeated.

"Yes," he said, "and Melissa is eager to meet you, by the way. She's delighted she's not the only girl in the family anymore."

"I'm the only girl in my family, too—" Erica laughed shortly as she looked at him. "But then, apparently I'm not."

An icy wind blasted down the street and the sun slipped behind a bank of gray clouds. Erica shivered, but didn't know if it was the emotional reaction or the sudden drop in temperature that caused it.

Christian said, "Don met your mother at a vulnerable point in his life—"

"And that excuses him?"

"No, it doesn't," he said, his features tightening even as his voice grew clipped. "I'm simply trying to explain it to you the same way Don did for me. He knew how you'd feel hearing this news."

"I'm surprised he gave it a thought," she said. "Not one word from him my whole life and now I'm supposed to be grateful that my biological father is popping up after his death?"

"He didn't contact you because he thought it would make your life more difficult."

"Putting it lightly."

"Exactly. Don't think you weren't on his mind,

though." Christian folded his hands around his coffee cup. "I knew him for a lot of years and I can tell you that to him, family was most important. It must have driven him insane knowing you were here and completely out of his reach."

"So my father's—Walter's—threat worked. Donald stayed away from me to avoid scandal."

"No." Christian smiled a little at that. "Don wasn't worried about what other people thought of him. My guess is he stayed away out of respect for you and your father. He wasn't the kind of man to go out looking to destroy marriages."

"And yet…"

Christian shook his head. "Just before he died, Don talked to me about all of this because he knew I'd be the one coming to see you."

"So even when he knew he was dying, he didn't get in touch with me." Erica wasn't sure how she felt about that. If Donald Jarrod had contacted her, would she have believed him? Would she have welcomed him? She couldn't say. Her relationship with her father had never been a good one, but she did love Walter. He *was* her father. The only one she'd ever known.

Didn't she at least owe him loyalty?

Frowning, the man across from her admitted, "I argued with him about that. I thought he should talk to you. Tell you this himself. But he refused to go back on his word. He'd sworn to Walter he would stay away and he did, though I believe it cost him a great deal to keep that promise."

"I'll have to take your word for that, won't I?"

"I guess so." Their waiter appeared with a coffeepot to refill Christian's cup, but when he would have stayed to take their order, he was waved away again. "Look," Christian continued when they were alone again. "Just do me a favor and read the last letter in that envelope before I say any more."

She really didn't want to. What more was there to tell? What in her life was left to shake up and rearrange? Yet, morbid curiosity had a grip on her now and Erica knew she'd have to satisfy it.

Somehow, she wasn't surprised when she glanced at the bottom of the page and saw the name *Donald Jarrod* in a bold signature. Lifting her gaze to the top of the paper, she read,

My Dear Erica,
I know how you must be feeling right now and I can't blame you. But please know that if I had been given the opportunity, I would have loved you as I cared for your mother.

People—even parents—aren't perfect. We make mistakes. But if we get the chance we try to correct them. This is my chance. Come to Colorado. Meet your other family. And one day, I hope you'll be able to think of me kindly.
Your father,
Donald Jarrod

Again her eyes misted over. She had never known her mother. She'd grown up with a stepmother, Angela, who had been as distant in her own way as Walter had. Now, it turned out, she'd never known her father, either.

"Did you read these letters?"

"No. Don gave them to me in the closed envelope and they've stayed sealed up until just now."

She looked at him. "And I'm supposed to take your word for that, too?"

He met her gaze. "I'll never lie to you, Erica. That is one thing you can depend on."

Since she'd only just discovered that her entire life had been based on a lie, that should have been a comforting statement. On the other hand, she didn't know if the statement itself was a lie.

A headache burst into life behind her eyes and Erica knew it was only going to get worse. So it was best if she just finished this meeting as quickly as possible. Then she could get away. Think. Plan. Try to make some sense out of this insensible situation.

Pushing her hair out of her eyes as the wind whipped it into a frenzy, she said, "All right. Say I believe you. I'm Donald Jarrod's daughter. What now?"

He reached down for his briefcase, opened it and extracted the manila envelope he'd shown her earlier. "As a beneficiary of Don's will, you receive an equal share of his estate."

"What?"

He gave her a small smile. "The estate's been split between all six of his children."

Erica sighed and took a gulp of her iced tea. "I can imagine how news of me went over at the reading of the will."

"As you might guess. Surprise. Shock."

"Sounds like we'll have a lot in common," she said wryly, still reeling from the information overload she'd experienced.

"More than you might think," he told her as he slid the envelope across the table toward her. "There's a catch to your inheritance, though."

"Of course there is," she mused, laying her fingertips atop the will as if she needed the physical contact to assure herself that this was all for real.

"Each of you has to move to Aspen to help run the family business. If you don't…"

"If we don't, then no inheritance."

"Basically."

"Move to Aspen?" She glanced around her at the city she'd grown up in and loved. The city sidewalks were at the bottom of canyons built of steel and brick. Sly sunlight poking through gray clouds appeared and disappeared as if performing magic tricks. Crowds of pedestrians hustled along, everyone hurrying, fighting the wind and the snarls of traffic. Car horns blared, music from a street corner musician peeled out and somewhere close by, a tiny dog yapped impatiently.

The city was hers.

What did she know about Colorado?

But was that even the point? How could she *not* go? Yet, if she did, how would her father and brothers react?

Christian watched her features and knew just by looking at her that her thoughts were tumultuous. Why wouldn't they be, though? He'd known that what he'd had to say to her would shake the foundations of her life. Make her question everything she had ever known.

And he still resented the hell out of the fact that Donald had left this mess in *his* hands.

"You don't have to make any decisions right now," he said after a few long minutes had passed.

She gave him a reluctant, halfhearted smile. "That's good, because I don't think I could."

Nodding, Christian offered, "Why don't you take a few days? Make your decision, then call me." He scribbled his cell number on the back of his business card, then handed it to her. "According to the will, you've got a couple of weeks to take up your place at the resort. Use the time. Think about what you want to do."

She held his card and ran her thumb over the embossed lettering in a slow stroke that mesmerized Christian. His body stirred and he shifted uncomfortably on his chair. He didn't need this attraction to her and wished he could shut it all down.

Unfortunately, the longer he was with her, the stronger that attraction became. What he'd like to do was blow off the business talk, take her for an elegant meal and then off to his hotel where he could lay her down across his bed and they could spend a couple of hours enjoying themselves. If she was any other woman, that's exactly what he would do.

That thought made him even more uncomfortable than he had been before.

Erica Prentice was off-limits and if she ended up going

to Aspen—which he thought she would—then his body had better get used to living with disappointment.

"A decision," she said softly, locking her gaze with his. "We both know what that decision will be."

"I think I do," he told her. "You're going to accept the conditions of the will."

"How can I not?"

He smiled in approval. "You have more of your father in you than you know."

"Which one?" she asked.

"Does it matter?" he countered.

Christian studied the woman across from him and tried once again to take a mental step back from the raging lust pounding through him. He'd never had such an immediate reaction to any woman before, and it was disconcerting as hell when he was trying to concentrate on business.

Her face was an open book. Every emotion she felt was written there for the world to see and he had to admit that he liked that about her. There were no artifices. What you saw with Erica Prentice was what you got.

She was strong, as well. The kind of news he'd just delivered might have flattened most women, but she was already finding a way to deal with it. Might not be easy, but he didn't think she was the kind of woman to run from a challenge. Her whiskey-colored eyes shone with tears she refused to shed and that, too, struck a spark of admiration in him. She could control her emotions, which would be good once she hit Aspen.

Dealing with a whole new family wouldn't be easy,

but he was willing to bet she'd make it work. But he had to wonder how the Jarrod siblings were going to handle it. They'd all been shocked of course, but he'd expected that. He hadn't counted on the outright hostility he'd sensed from Blake and Guy. If they tried taking their outrage at their father out on Erica, Christian would just have to stop them.

Surprised at the thought, he realized that he was feeling...protective of her. Which didn't make a bit of sense since he'd only just met her. But there it was. She'd had her whole life turned upside down and inside out and damned if he'd let the Jarrod twins make her feel even worse about it.

"Is there something else you're not telling me?"

He looked at Erica. "What? No. Why do you ask?"

"Because you suddenly looked fierce enough to bite through steel."

"Oh." Apparently his legendary poker face, his ability to mask his emotions, was slipping today. "No, it's nothing. I was just thinking about some business I have to take care of back in Aspen."

"Right. You live there, too."

"I do." He smiled to himself, thinking about the home he had built on the Jarrod property. "I've got a house on the resort grounds. Don wanted his lawyer close by."

"Handy."

"It has been." He shrugged and expanded on that a little. "I grew up in Aspen. Worked at the Jarrod Resort as a teenager."

"So you knew my—" she stopped and rephrased what she'd been about to say "—Don Jarrod a long time."

"Since I was a kid."

"So you know his children, too."

"Sure. We didn't hang out together as kids, but I knew them. Got to know them better later on."

"What're they like?"

"You know," he said, glancing around for the waiter that had apparently given up on them ordering lunch, "we should get a meal while we talk."

"I'm not hungry, thanks."

"Oh." He should have figured she'd still be too shaken to eat. "Are you sure?"

"I am. Just tell me how they took this news. Are they furious? Am I going to be facing a firing squad in Colorado?"

He gave her a smile he hoped was reassuring. "Nothing so dramatic. I admit they were as stunned as you. But they're nice people. They'll deal with it."

She took a deep breath and blew it out again. "I suppose we'll all have to."

There it was, he thought, that thread of steel running through her slender, feminine body. "I have to say, I'm surprised at how well you're taking this. I actually expected you to need more convincing."

She shook her head and thought about that for a moment before answering. When she did, her voice was soft and low. "I've just discovered that my entire life has been built on lies." Her eyes met his and Christian felt the power of her stare slam into him. "I have to know the truth. I don't expect you to understand this, but I feel as though I *have* to go. Not for the inheritance. I don't need Don Jarrod's money. I have to go for *me*. I have to find out who I really am."

He had the oddest urge to reach across the table and cover her hand with his. His palm actually burned to touch her, but he resisted, somehow knowing that one touch would be both too much and not enough. Instead, he kept his voice deliberately businesslike as he said, "I do understand. You need to see *both* of your lives to be able to accept either one."

She tipped her head to one side and studied him. "You do understand." After a long moment, she turned her head to look out at the street pulsing with life behind them. "Until this morning, I thought my life was pretty dull. Routine. The biggest problem facing me this morning was getting through the morning meeting at the office. Now, I don't know what to think."

"Maybe you should give yourself a break. Don't try to figure anything out yet." He saw confusion and hurt in her eyes and he didn't like the fact that it bothered him. "All I'm saying is, wait. Go to Aspen. Meet your other family. Take some time."

She nodded thoughtfully. "Before I can do that, I have to go see my father," she said. "I need to hear what he has to say about this."

"Of course." He stood up as she did and held out one hand toward her. When she slid her palm against his, heat skittered up the length of his arm to reverberate through his chest. Oh, yes, touching her was an invitation to disaster. Instantly, he released her hand again. "I'll be flying back to Aspen tomorrow, so if you have any other questions, I'm at the Hyatt at the Embarcadero."

She smiled. "I love that hotel. Good choice."

"Nice view of the bay," he admitted. As she picked up her purse and the manila envelopes he'd given her, Christian heard himself say, "Call me when you're ready to come to Colorado. I'll tell you what to expect when you arrive."

"I will." She swung her purse up onto her shoulder, held on to the manila envelopes he'd given her and said, "I guess I'll be seeing you again soon, then."

"Soon." He nodded and stood there alone to watch her leave. Sunlight slanted through a bank of clouds and dazzled her hair with light. Her hips swayed and his gaze fixed on her behind so he could enjoy the view.

The next time he saw her, they would be in Aspen. Surrounded by the Jarrod family, he would be forced to keep his distance from her, and Christian didn't like the thought of that at all. He had a feeling that cleaning up the mess Don had left behind was going to be a lot harder than he'd believed it would be.

Three

Erica was always nervous when she walked into the headquarters of the Prentice Group. Of course, that was the impression her father wanted to make on prospective clients or competitors. Walter wanted people to be intimidated by their surroundings, because then he would always have the psychological advantage.

The building itself was massive, a glass-and-steel tower. Its tinted windows kept the sun at bay and prevented prying eyes in neighboring buildings from peeking in. As if that weren't enough, the décor had all the warmth and comfort of the great man himself. Cold tile, white walls and stiff, modernistic furniture set the scene in the main lobby and that tone was echoed on every floor.

Walter Prentice was a firm believer in the saying

"Perception is everything." He showed the world what he wanted them to see and that picture became reality. Erica thought about her father—or the man she'd always considered her father—for a second and felt an old ripple of anger slide beneath the surface of the confusion and hurt rampaging through her.

She'd been raised to uphold the family name. To be a shining beacon of respectability and decorum. This building was the heartbeat of the Prentice family dynasty. Where her brothers worked with their father. Where family meetings she was never included in were held. Where the men of the family made plans that the women were expected to follow. This was the place she had never felt good enough to enter.

Her father hadn't wanted her here. He'd made that clear enough. Wouldn't even consider her working in the family business, no matter how she had tried to convince him. Erica had never understood why, but she had been on the outside looking in for most of her life. Today, she had discovered the reasons behind her sense of seclusion.

Did her older brothers know the truth? Was that why they'd never really been close? As a kid, she'd wondered why her big brothers weren't like those of her friends. Sure, they were much older than she was, but still, they'd never paid attention to her. They'd never had the kind of relationship she had once wished for. Had they known the truth all along? Was she the only one who'd been in the dark?

It was time to find out.

She walked across the gleaming, cream-colored tile

floor to the security desk. The general public could just walk up to the bank of elevators on the south wall and take them up to any number of floors. But to reach the top floor, where her father's and brothers' offices were, required a stop at security where you were given a badge that would get you onto the penthouse elevator. As a child, she'd always felt "special" going through these motions. Today, she only felt even less a part of the Prentice world.

"Good afternoon, Ms. Prentice."

"Hi, Jerry," she said. The older man had been working in her father's lobby for twenty years. When she was a child, Erica remembered, Jerry had kept candy at his station so he always had some for her when she arrived. Now that she thought about it, she realized Jerry had always been happier to see her than Walter had. "I'm going up to see my father."

"That's good. Nice for a father and daughter to stay close," he said as he made a notation in his log, then handed her a badge. "Now that my Karen's moved out to college I don't see her nearly enough."

Erica smiled and hoped it looked more convincing than it felt. Fathers and daughters. She wondered wistfully if Don Jarrod had been a good father. Had her sister, Melissa, had the kind of connection with her father that Erica had always hungered for? Or had her biological father been cut from the same cloth as Walter? After all, they were both wealthy, important men. Maybe it was in their natures to be closed off and more concerned with business than with their children.

Some relationships were so much closer than others. And some, she mused, with a thought for the father she would never know, were never realized at all.

"You have a nice day now," Jerry said as she took the badge and headed for the private elevator.

Nice day. Two words rattling around inside her mind as she pushed the call button. Confusing day. Terrifying day. Nice? Not so much. In seconds, the doors swished open, she stepped inside and listened to the muted music that drifted down around her.

Now that she was here, Erica's stomach was churning. What was she going to say? What *could* she say? "Hello, Father, or should I call you Walter?"

Tears stung at her eyes, but she blinked them back. She hadn't cried in front of Christian Hanford and she wouldn't cry now. For one brief moment, the Colorado attorney's gorgeous face rose up in her mind and Erica thought if only he hadn't been there to tear down the foundations of her life, she would have been seriously attracted to him. But it was hard to notice a hum in your body when your heart was breaking.

Even now, her heart hurt and her knees were trembling. Music played on as the elevator silently streamed skyward. She should have thought this through more before coming to the office, Erica told herself. Figured out what she was going to say before coming here. But her feelings had pushed her here. That wild rush of anger and confusion and hurt was simmering inside her and waiting wouldn't have made a difference. She wouldn't have calmed down. If anything, the tension riding her would have only increased with a wait.

Besides, she thought as the elevator stopped and the doors slid open to reveal the rarefied air of the penthouse suite of offices, it was too late to back out now. She was here and it was past time for answers.

Thick, cream-colored carpet stretched on forever. Her father didn't want to be bothered by the clipping sound of shoes on tile. And what Walter Prentice wanted, he got. So the carpet was thick and the music soft. It was like stepping into a cloud, she thought. The view out the glass walls was impressive, the city stretched out all around them and the bay just beyond.

Taking a deep breath, Erica walked down the long hall to the desk of her father's assistant. Jewel Franks was fiftyish, no-nonsense and had her fingers on the pulse of the entire company. She had iron-gray hair neatly coiffed, cool blue eyes and the patience of a saint. She had to, to be able to work with Walter on a daily basis as she had for the last thirty years.

"Erica!" Jewel smiled at her. "What a lovely surprise. Your father isn't expecting you, is he? I don't have you on my list for the day...."

Erica felt a reluctant smile curve her mouth. Jewel's lists were legendary. If it wasn't written on her legal pad, it didn't exist.

"No, I'm sorry," she said. "This is a spur-of-the-moment thing, Jewel. Does he have a few minutes?"

The older woman gave her a wink. "You just managed to catch him between calls, honey. Why don't you go on in?"

"Thanks." Erica's stomach spun and dipped, as if her insides were dizzy and looking for a way to sit down.

Another deep breath to fortify already flagging nerves and she was walking to the double-door entrance to her father's office. A soft knock, then she turned the brass knob and entered.

"What is it, Jewel?" Walter didn't even look up from the sheaf of papers on his desk.

Erica took a second to study him as he sat there. All of her life, she'd looked up to this man, tried to please him and wondered why she continually failed. His hair was thick and cut short, white mingling with the black now, and his navy blue suit fit him like a uniform. Which it was, she supposed, since she had rarely seen her father in anything but a suit and tie. That tie was power-red today and as he lifted his gaze to look at her, she saw his eyes narrow in question.

"Erica? What are you doing here?"

Not exactly a warm greeting, but Walter never had cared for being interrupted at the office. "Hello, Father."

Openly frowning now, he asked, "Is there something wrong? Shouldn't you be at work?"

She watched his face, searching for some sign of warmth or pleasure, but there was nothing. So she walked across the floor, never taking her eyes from his. When she was standing opposite his desk, she said, "I had a visitor today. A lawyer from Colorado."

Walter jerked as if he'd been shot. Then he stiffened in his chair and set his sterling silver pen onto the desk top. His features went deliberately blank.

"Colorado?" He repeated the word without the slightest inflection in his voice.

"Don't," Erica said, staring into those distant green eyes of his as she had her whole life, hoping to see love shining back at her. But again, she was disappointed. "Don't pretend to not know what I'm talking about."

His eyes narrowed as he sat back in his chair and gave an impatient tug to his suit vest. "Young lady, don't take that tone with me."

Erica almost laughed and would have if her heart wasn't aching in her chest. She hadn't heard that particular phrase from him since she was seventeen, and telling her father she was going to a concert with her friends. Of course, she hadn't gone to the concert, since he'd refused permission and sent her to her room. She wasn't a rebellious girl anymore though, fighting her own nerves and her father for the right to spread her wings. And she no longer needed his permission to do what she felt she had to do. She was all grown-up and she deserved some answers.

"Father," she said quietly, "the attorney told me some things. Things I need to talk to you about."

"I can imagine he did. But I'm not going to discuss this with you." His jaw jutted out, his eyes narrowed and he silently dared her to continue.

"I need to know, Father," she said, doing just that. "I have the right to hear it from you. I have to know if everything he said was true."

"You want to talk about rights? What about my rights to not have this distasteful matter resurrected?" he muttered, tapping his fingers against the desk in a nervous tattoo. "You're Erica Prentice. My daughter, and by heaven, that should be enough for you."

God, she wished it were. She wanted it to be enough. But just looking at Walter's face told her that there was so much more she needed to know. All her life, she'd loved this man. Wanted him to be proud of her. Had strived to be the best—at everything—just to win his approval.

Now, she wanted him to tell her this was all a mistake. Some cruel trick. Yet even before she'd come here, she'd known it wasn't. "Father, please. Talk to me. I don't even know what to think about all of this."

He ground his teeth together, his jaw working furiously before he said, "That bastard Jarrod. This is all his fault. Even from the grave he tries to steal from me."

"What?" That was not the opening she'd been expecting.

Walter pushed back from his desk and stood up. "He left orders in his will to contact you, didn't he?" He shoved one hand through his hair, startling Erica. It was the first time she'd ever seen him actually rattled.

"I knew he would," Walter was muttering. "It was the one sure way he could get around me. Should have known he wouldn't keep his word."

This was getting more confusing by the moment. "Don Jarrod left me an equal share in his estate."

Walter snorted derisively. "Of course he did. He knew I couldn't stop him and this was the only way he had left to stick it to me."

"To you?" Erica shook her head and felt the sting of tears she wouldn't allow burning in her eyes again. "This isn't about you, Father, this is about me."

"Don't you fool yourself." Walter stabbed his index finger at her. "This was always about Don Jarrod and what he could take from me. No better than a damn thief, that man."

Heart sinking in her chest, Erica watched as Walter's features went florid with the rush of temper. Even knowing it was foolish, she'd been harboring one small flicker of doubt inside her. The hope that this was all wrong. That Don Jarrod had made a mistake. That Walter was her father and really did love her. So much for hope.

"So he really was my father?"

"Yes." Walter bit the word off as if it had tasted foul. "The bastard." He glanced at her, then looked away again and stalked across the room to stare out at the gloomy view of gray sky and sea. "Your mother and I were having…problems. No point in getting into them now, it's over and done years ago. But we separated for a time. I went to England for several months, setting up the European branch of the company. Thought it best if Danielle and I each had some space. Some time to consider what we wanted."

She stared at his broad back as he kept his gaze fixed on the window and the world beyond the glass. He couldn't even look at her as he spoke and that ripped another tiny shred out of her heart.

He had thought it best to leave her mother for a while, Erica told herself and wondered what her mother's wishes had been. Then Walter was talking again and she paid attention.

"Don Jarrod was here, in town, supposedly buying

up a hotel or two. They met at the theater. Introduced by mutual friends," he said that last word with a sneer, as if the sting of betrayal were still too sharp. Then he inhaled deeply and exhaled on a rush of words. "The bastard took advantage of her. I was out of the country, and Jarrod saw she was vulnerable, sad. He romanced her, seduced her and got her pregnant."

Erica swayed unsteadily, but kept standing. It all sounded so awful. So…tacky. How was she supposed to feel about this? She was the unplanned result of a hurried affair. Not the sort of thing a woman wants to hear.

Walter was still talking. "Of course," he told her, with a glance over his shoulder, "I didn't realize your mother was expecting you until after we'd reconciled…."

That's when it hit her. "So you were separated when—" It didn't really make it better, but at least her mother hadn't been cheating.

"Hardly matters," Walter argued. "We were still married. Not that Don Jarrod would care about that. I loved my wife. I wanted our marriage back. Danielle assured me the affair was long over. Jarrod had returned to Colorado and we put it behind us. When she discovered she was pregnant, she went against my wishes and told him because she felt he had the right to know about his child."

"He knew all these years."

Walter snorted. "Yes. Naturally he got in contact. He wanted to be a part of your life—as if I would ever have allowed that. The scandal of it would have rocked this city. Ruined business, cost me clients. I couldn't have that."

"Of course not," she whispered, feeling another sharp slice of pain. Scandal was the one thing Walter wouldn't tolerate. The idea of his friends and business associates knowing about his wife's affair would have been unbearable for him. He hadn't hidden the truth because of his desire to protect and love her, but to save himself embarrassment.

This explained a lot, she told herself, her mind racing, darting from one thought to the next so quickly she could hardly keep up. As a girl, she had dreamed of a daddy who doted on her. After all, she was the youngest in the family by quite a bit. The youngest of her older brothers was still fifteen years older than she. Erica had grown up practically an only child. Her brothers were out and building lives of their own by the time she was a teenager.

But Walter had never been the kind of father she'd yearned for. At last, she knew why. And Erica wondered sadly if Don Jarrod would have been any different. He was—or had been—much like Walter, a businessman first last and always.

And yet…

"He wanted me," she said softly, more to herself than to Walter.

"He wanted to ruin *me*," Walter told her flatly. Some of the hot color drained from his features. "He tried to convince your mother to leave me. Go with him to that backwater out in the country. But she knew what was best. What was right." He nodded with satisfaction. "Besides, I told her I wouldn't hold her mistake against her."

"No," Erica said softly. "You held it against me."

He stared at her. "I beg your pardon?"

Erica's pain was enveloped by a rising tide of regret and sadness. "Father, my whole life you've looked at me with barely concealed revulsion."

"Not true," he said, but his gaze slipped to one side, avoiding her eyes.

Even now, he couldn't look at her. Couldn't meet her gaze and admit to the truth. But she wouldn't play the game anymore. She finally understood why she'd always been a little less worthy than her brothers and that in itself was liberating.

"Yes," she said, "it is. I used to wonder what I'd done that was so wrong. So awful to make you dislike me so much."

"I don't dislike you, Erica," he said, surprise coloring his voice. "I love you."

She wished she could believe that, but with her heart aching it was simply impossible. "You've never acted as if you do."

He squared his shoulders and lifted his chin. "I'm not an emotional man, Erica, but you should be well aware of my feelings."

"Until this moment, I wasn't sure you had any," Erica snapped, then lifted one hand to cover her mouth, almost as stunned as he was that she'd said such a thing.

He looked at her as if she was someone he didn't even recognize, and to be fair, Erica thought, she could understand his reaction. In her whole life, she'd never once spoken back to him this way. Stood up for herself. Always, she had tried to be the perfect daughter. To win a smile or a nod of approval from him. At this moment though, none of that meant anything to her. Right now, all she felt was her own hurt. Her own disappointment. Her own wish that things were different.

"Erica," he said, that deep voice rumbling out around her as it had since her childhood. "I *am* your father in every way that matters. Haven't I always been here for you? Didn't I raise you? Have you *ever* wanted for anything?"

"Only your love," she said, voice catching as she finally admitted to him that she'd felt that lack her whole life.

"How can you say that?" His shocked expression told her exactly how surprised he was by her words.

The tears that she'd managed to hold at bay all day finally began to show themselves. Irritated by their arrival, Erica quickly swiped them away with the backs of her hands.

"I'm sorry, Father," she said at last. "Maybe my coming here wasn't a good idea. I didn't want to upset you. Didn't want us to tear at each other."

He took a single step toward her, then stopped, clearly unsure of his next move. Which was, she thought, another first.

"Erica…" He paused as if gathering his scattered thoughts, then said, "Your mother wouldn't want you to go. She'd want you to stay here. With your family."

Would she? Erica wondered. Or would her mother understand the need to discover her roots? God, what a clichéd way to think of this. But wasn't it true? Wouldn't she be exploring her past so that she could figure out her future?

"I do love you, Father," she told him. "But I'm going to Colorado. I have to. To meet my brothers and sister. To find out if I belong there any more than I do here."

"What's *that* supposed to mean?" His bellow was completely unexpected. Walter Prentice never lost his temper. Or at least, he'd never allowed anyone to witness it. "Of course you belong here, this is your home. We're your family."

"So are they."

"You will not do this thing." He folded his arms across his chest. "I forbid it."

Erica had to smile through her tears. Typical of this man, she thought. If he couldn't sway, he would command, fully expecting that his opposition would fold and do exactly as he wanted.

Still, she loved him and wished he would sweep her up into his big arms and tell her this was all nonsense. That of course he loved her. Always had. Always would. She wanted to be cuddled against her father's broad chest and reassured about her place in the world.

But that wasn't going to happen.

Sadly, she faced him. "You can't stop me, Father, so please don't try." Erica walked to the door and opened it but before she could slip through, his voice halted her.

"If you don't find what you're looking for there?" he asked. "What then?"

She glanced back at him and suddenly thought that he looked so...lonely, in his plush office surrounded by the symbols of his success. "Honestly? I just don't know."

"So what is she like?"

Christian looked up from the desk in his office at the Manor and smiled at Melissa Jarrod. She wore a pale yellow silk blouse tucked into a short, dark green skirt. Her heeled sandals gave her already five-foot-eight height three extra inches and her blue eyes were sparkling with excitement. She shook her long fall of blond hair back from her face, planted both hands on the desktop and leaned toward him.

Looked as though he wouldn't be getting much work done, he told himself. Melissa was bound and determined to get information on her new sister and until he surrendered to the inevitable, Christian knew the woman wouldn't be going anywhere.

"Come on, Christian, give a little," she prodded.

"I already told you she seems very nice," he said.

"Nice doesn't tell me a lot." She straightened up and paced around the room. "Is she funny? Boring?"

He didn't remember her being boring, Christian thought. Would have been easier on him if she had been. But no, Erica Prentice had to be strong and intelligent and—not helping, he told himself. "She's...nice."

Melissa laughed. "Honestly, you're hopeless. You make a terrible spy."

"Good thing I'm a lawyer then," he said and shifted his gaze back to the papers on the desk. His brief hope that he'd satisfied her curiosity and would be allowed to get back to work was shattered a second later.

"Fine. As a lawyer, give me a description. Tell me how she reacted. What she's thinking. Something," she begged.

Sitting back in his chair, Christian looked across the room at the youngest Jarrod sibling—well, now thanks to Erica, she was the second youngest. Melissa hadn't taken long at all to decide to come home to Aspen. She'd quit her job managing a trendy, luxurious day spa in Los Angeles and had taken over at the spa here at the resort. Since she was also a yoga instructor, she had plans to include yoga retreats at the spa, as well. She'd slipped back into mountain life as if she'd never left it.

"What do you want to hear?"

"I don't know," she said, laughing again. "I have a sister I've never met. Is she fun? Does she smile a lot? Is she stuffy? You know, more into business than anything else? Because really, with my brothers, I'm hoping she's not."

"She didn't seem to be," he said, thinking back on that one day he'd had with Erica. Not like he hadn't been doing a lot of thinking about her ever since they first met. On the long flight home, he'd almost convinced himself that the instant attraction he'd felt for her wasn't as overwhelming as he'd believed. But then Erica had called him that night to tell him she would be arriving in just a few days.

All it had taken was hearing her voice and his body was tight and hard and… Christian cut those thoughts off fast. Melissa was pretty damned intuitive and he didn't need her picking up on what he was feeling for her sister.

"She was," he said, before Melissa could prod him again, "surprised. As shocked as all of you were to hear about her connection to the family."

"Poor thing," Melissa murmured, her soft heart showing. "I can't even imagine having that curve ball thrown at you."

"You did have it thrown at you," he reminded her.

"Yeah, but I already knew I was a Jarrod. She's coming into this cold and it had to be hard to find out you're not who you think you are."

Christian smiled at her again. She was going to be an ally for Erica. A safe harbor in a strange new world. And that was a good thing. He had a feeling she was going to need friends. In their communications with him, Blake and Guy weren't exactly warming up to the idea of a new sister. And as for Gavin and Trevor…he'd know when they arrived what their attitude was going to be.

"I think it's safe to say it hit her hard. She's strong though," Christian told her. "Every bit as tough as you are. But she's got a soft side, too," he mused, remembering the sheen of tears she'd managed to keep at bay when they'd been talking.

"Do I detect some interest there?" Melissa asked.

"What?" He straightened up and glared at her. Damn it, he couldn't afford to relax his guard for a minute around her. She was way too perceptive. "No. You don't. Besides, that would be inappropriate."

"Oh, for heaven's sake, Christian," Melissa said with a sad shake of her head, "you sound like a Puritan or something."

"I'm not and I'm also not discussing this with you. Don't you have a spa to run?"

Frustrated, she huffed out a breath. "Honestly, men are the most bizarre creatures."

"Thanks so much. Goodbye."

"Oh, I'm going," she said, smiling now as she headed for his office door. "But don't think this ends the conversation, Christian."

Once she was gone, he leaned back in his chair again and told himself to shape up. He couldn't afford to show any of the Jarrod siblings that he was attracted to Erica. With the board of directors due to meet in a few months, he couldn't afford to start rumors.

Dating a member of the Jarrod family was one sure way for an employee to find himself quickly unemployed. It was there in the contracts they all signed, since Don had been adamant about protecting his family. Don's will ensured that the fraternization clause would stay. The board of directors would follow Don's directions until new ones were put in their place. Christian couldn't count on the Jarrod siblings doing anything to change the status quo. And he wasn't going to give up the job he'd worked so hard for and loved so much for any woman.

No matter how much he wanted her.

Four

Three days after her lunch with Christian, Erica was on a private plane headed to Aspen. Strange how quickly she'd managed to pull this together. Erica had taken a leave of absence from her firm, closed up her condo and put her car into storage. When she called Christian Hanford to tell him her plans, he'd insisted on sending the family jet for her. She'd argued with him of course, but Erica thought as she looked around her, she was glad she'd lost that argument.

The plane was furnished with both elegance and comfort in mind. Thick, sky-blue carpeting covered the floor and the dozen seats were in pale blue leather and more comfy than any first-class accommodation she'd ever tried. There was a flat-screen TV on the bulkhead, a selection of movies for the DVD player and a stereo outfitted with dozens of CDs. There was also a uniformed hostess who had served Erica a delicious breakfast before disappearing into the front of the plane with the pilot and copilot.

She had the cabin to herself and Erica was grateful for the respite. She'd been doing so much thinking and considering over the last few days, had had so many people talking to her and at her, it was nearly a vacation to have some quiet time to herself.

Although, with all of this quality thinking time, she was starting to make herself crazy wondering what exactly she was getting herself into. Christian had said that her new family was eager to meet her.

She had to wonder about that. He was probably just being nice. Why would they be taking this situation any better than her older brothers had? She hardly saw her siblings unless it was at some family function, but only the day before, the three of them had descended on her en masse to try to talk her out of this move.

Erica leaned her head back against the seat and closed her eyes. She could still hear her brothers' voices, alternately pleading, arguing and demanding that she stop hurting the man who'd loved her and raised her. Strange how they were all so interested in protecting Walter from a truth he'd known all along. None of them had given much thought to what *she* was having to deal with.

Even with her brothers coming at her from all sides, that confrontation hadn't been as bad as the one with her stepmother. Angela, to give the woman her due, loved Walter to distraction. She'd made him happy,

Erica knew, and she'd even tried, in the beginning, to foster a relationship with Erica. But the woman really wasn't very maternal and Erica had been old enough to resent a woman who wasn't her mother trying to take over her life. So they'd never really connected. And that wasn't likely to change now, she thought as she remembered that last scene with her stepmother.

"You're hurting him with this, Erica," Angela had said softly, *her tone and expression clearly showing her disapproval. "He doesn't deserve this sort of treatment from you."*

"Angela, all I want to do is find out who I am," she argued patiently.

"And you believe your father resents your choice."

"Are you saying he doesn't?"

Angela took a long breath and let it sigh from her lungs. Picking up her clutch, she tucked it beneath her left arm and slowly shook her head. "You've never looked past his brusque exterior to the man beneath, have you?" Not waiting for an answer, she said, "One day you will, my dear. And you'll see that Walter's heart aches for you. He loves you, Erica. It doesn't matter that Don Jarrod donated his sperm to your creation. It's Walter Prentice who is your father."

Was Angela right? Or was she only defending her husband as she always had? Erica didn't know, but she couldn't allow anything to stop her from this quest.

"So basically," Erica whispered to no one, "I'm on my own. Probably about time, too," she added under her breath.

Heaven knew this was the greatest adventure she'd ever undertaken. Unlike her friends, she hadn't backpacked through Europe after graduating from college. She hadn't taken a year off to "find" herself. Instead, she'd done exactly what was expected of her. She had gotten a job at a well-regarded firm and began the process of building a respectable life. In fact, Erica had never done a single thing on impulse. She had been the good little girl, doing the right thing. The proper thing. All because she had been trying to prove herself to a father who had never noticed her. Now though, it seemed she was making up for all of that.

Pulling up stakes and moving halfway across the country to live with people she didn't know and help run a resort she'd never seen.

It was crazy. Made zero sense. She should be terrified.

But she wasn't.

Erica looked out the window at the earth far below and watched the view change from city to mountains and plains and felt a stir of excitement rise up inside her. This was new. Fresh. She had a chance here that few people ever had. An opportunity to completely reinvent herself. She was going to do the best she could with it. She was going to find her way and figure out who she was and when that was done, she'd be able to face her father again and hold her head high.

She picked up her cup of coffee and sipped at it. But for the muffled roar of the engines, the inside of the jet was quiet. She wasn't interested in watching a movie or listening to the selection of music they had on board. In fact, she was actually too restless to sit still. The only thing keeping her in her buttery-soft leather chair was her instinctive fear of flying. And as the time ticked away, Erica's excitement turned into nervousness and she worried about the reception she'd be receiving once she landed.

Friends? Or enemies? And how would she be able to tell?

The pilot's voice crackled over the speaker, interrupting her thoughts. "Ms. Prentice, please make sure your seat belt is fastened. We're beginning our initial descent and will be landing in Aspen in about twenty minutes."

She nodded as if the man could see her, then smiled at herself.

Only twenty minutes until her new life started.

He was waiting on the tarmac.

Christian Hanford looked different than he had in San Francisco, Erica thought as her heartbeat sped into a gallop. For one thing, he wasn't wearing a suit. And if she'd thought him gorgeous in that elegantly cut business suit, it was nothing to how she felt now.

He was wearing dark blue jeans, black boots and a red pullover collared shirt. His short dark hair ruffled in the wind and his lazy stance as he leaned against a black BMW only added to the "dangerous" air about him.

He walked to meet her as she came down the retractable stairway. A half smile on his face, he stopped at the bottom of the staircase and looked up at her. "How was your trip?"

"Fabulous," she said quickly. "Thank you for sending the jet for me."

"Least we could do," he said and held out one hand to help her down the last few steps. His thumb traced lightly over the back of her hand and his touch felt like licks of flame. His dark eyes locked with hers and Erica felt a nearly magnetic pull toward the man. For one split second it was as if they were the only two people in the world. His square jaw was shadowed with a faint trace of whiskers and his mouth was still curved in that half smile as he added, "It's the Jarrod family jet. You're family."

She laid her free hand against her abdomen in an attempt to still the butterflies that had suddenly decided to swarm inside her. It was a wasted effort. With excitement came nerves and she didn't expect either to let up anytime soon.

"How about a quick tour of Aspen before we go to the resort?"

"I'd like that," she said, tearing her gaze from his really gorgeous dark chocolate eyes long enough to look around her. Once she did, she gasped.

She glanced around the small—compared to San Francisco—airport and the mountains surrounding them. The sky was so blue it nearly hurt to look at it and the white clouds scudding across that sky could have been painted on, they were so perfect. The air was sharp and clean and the relative quiet was nearly deafening to a woman used to the sounds of a city.

"It's beautiful," she whispered, staring out at the mountains that towered over them like guardian angels.

"You know," he said, and she turned to catch him looking at her, "it really is." Then he shook off whatever he was thinking, and gave her hand a tug. "Come on, city girl. Let me show you around."

She was too damn beautiful; that was the problem, Christian told himself. He'd hoped that his memory of her was exaggerated. That she hadn't really had eyes the color of finely aged whiskey. That she didn't smell like peaches. That her softly layered hair didn't really lift in the wind until it looked like a halo around her head. He'd hoped that his desire for her would be something he could tuck away and ignore.

But just touching her hand had set off explosions of want inside him and now Christian knew exactly what he was up against.

Temptation.

He kept her hand tucked into his as he led her toward his car. The top was down and it was a perfect day for her to see her new home. When he opened the car door for her he took an extra second to enjoy the view. She wore white linen slacks, a dark blue shirt and black leather flats, and managed to look more beautiful than any woman had a right to. Oh, yeah. He was in deep trouble.

He closed the car door and said, "We'll drive through town, let you get your bearings."

"What about my luggage?"

"They'll deliver it to the resort."

"Right." She nodded. "Okay then."

He hopped in on the driver's side, fired the engine and drove out of the airport.

"I can't believe the mountains are so close," she said, pushing her windblown hair out of her face.

"I've lived here my whole life so I guess I don't really take the time to look up at them much."

"I don't know how you could do anything else," she admitted.

He followed her gaze briefly, allowing himself to admire the sweep of green that climbed up the mountains ringing Aspen. Like most citizens of Aspen, he more or less took the natural beauty of the place for granted. When you grew up in the middle of a painting, you tended to think everyone else lived with those kinds of views, too.

Christian gave her a quick grin. "I give you two weeks before you stop noticing them, just like the rest of us."

She glanced at him and shook her head. "I'll take that bet."

As he drove into the city, he rattled off the names of the businesses crowded along the streets. On Galena he pointed out the old brick buildings, several of the shops and Erica noticed the flower boxes lining the walkways between stores. Down Main Street, he showed her the *Aspen Times,* one of the town newspapers, and she smiled at the small blue building adorned with old-fashioned gold lettering across the front.

He knew what she was seeing, but he had to admit

that like the mountains, he tended to take for granted the charm of the city he'd grown up in.

It was modern of course, with plenty of high-end boutiques and shops for the megawealthy and celebrities who flocked here every year. But it was also an old mining town. Brick buildings, narrow streets, brightly colored flowers in boxes and old-fashioned light posts that were more atmospheric than useful. It was a mingling of three centuries, he supposed.

"In Aspen, we've sort of held on to the old while we welcomed the new."

"I love it," she said, her head whipping from side to side so she could take it all in.

He threw a quick look at her, saw pure pleasure dancing in her eyes and wondered how he was going to maintain a strictly business relationship with the youngest of Don's daughters. As his mind wrestled with his body's wants, he tried to focus on the road and not the way she lazily crossed her legs.

"It's so big," she said after another minute or two.

"Aspen?" He gave her another quick look. Coming from a city the size of San Francisco, he was surprised to hear she thought Aspen was big. "It's not, really. Population's around five thousand with a hell of a lot more than that every winter for the skiing and in the summer for the food and wine gala."

"No, not Aspen itself," she corrected. "Colorado. It's all so…open. God, the sky just goes on forever." She laughed a little and shrugged. "I'm more used to fragments of sky outlined by office buildings."

"Which do you like better?"

"Well," she said as he stopped at a red light, "that's the question, isn't it? San Francisco is beautiful, but in a completely different way. I feel so out of my element here."

The light changed, he put the car in gear and stepped on the gas. Keeping his eyes on the road, he said, "You're Don Jarrod's daughter, so Colorado's in your blood. Your family goes back a long way here."

"Tell me," she said, focusing on him now more than the city around them.

"I'll do my best," he said, thinking back to everything he'd heard Don talking about over the years. "Don's great-great-grandfather started the resort. He was here for the silver mining boom that started the city back in 1879. Bought himself some land and built what he called the biggest, damnedest house in Colorado."

Erica smiled. "No shortage of self-esteem in the Jarrod family then?"

"Not at all," Christian agreed with a chuckle. "Anyway, by 1893, Aspen had banks, theaters, a hospital and electric lights."

"Impressive," she said, half turning in her seat to watch him as he spoke.

"It was. Then the bottom dropped out of the silver market, mines closed and people moved out by the hundreds. Eli Jarrod refused to go, though. He kept adding on to his house, and opened it up as a hotel. There were still plenty of people back east who wanted to come out here on fishing and hunting trips and Eli was set up to take care of them."

"Smart."

"Not a shortage of brains in the Jarrod family, either," he told her. "Anyway, Eli managed to hang on. The Depression wasn't easy for anybody, but then the resort really took off in 1946. Then people were discovering the mountains for skiing and the Jarrods were prepared to handle the tourism trade."

"Right place, right time?"

"I guess," he said, "though they hung on through the lean years when everyone said that a hotel in the middle of 'nowhere' was a bad idea. So maybe you could just put their success down to pure stubbornness."

He steered the car past a delivery truck and along street after street. Businesses gave way to bungalow homes set far back on wide lots dotted with pines. Soon they left the city behind and turned onto a road guarded on either side by tall trees and open space.

"Tell me about the resort."

Christian nodded. "Like I said, it started out as just the family home, though your ancestor made sure it was the biggest house for miles around. As he turned it into a hotel, the place got even grander. Wings were added off the main building and the Jarrod resort was born." He took a sharp left and steered the car across the bridge spanning the Roaring Fork River. "And the resort just kept growing. The main hotel is out front and the top floor is the family residence. That's where you'll be staying."

She took a breath and nodded. "Okay, what else?"

"There are lodges built on the grounds, some of them actually going up the slope of the mountain. There are standard log cabins, some stone ones. Most of the lodges are small and cozy, one-family deals, but there are much bigger ones too, fully staffed with butlers, maids and cooks."

Her eyebrows rose. "Wow."

"Oh, yeah." He steered the car down a narrow road lined with stands of trees so thick she could barely see through them. "I think you're about to be amazed, Erica Prentice."

She laughed. "What makes you think I haven't been already?"

"It's about to get better," he assured her.

The long drive up to the resort unfolded in front of them. An acre of neatly tended lawn bordered by banks of flowers spilling color and scent lay in front of the truly impressive Manor.

Erica felt her mouth drop open. "It's a castle," she whispered, her gaze sweeping up and over the main stone building, then encompassing the wings jutting out from either side. Flowering green shrubs crouched at the base of the Manor and gleaming window panes shone in the sun like diamonds. There were peaked roofs, balconies with iron railings and the aged brick of the structure itself was the color of roses.

It would have seemed like a postcard, but for the bustle of employees around the circular drive making the whole place come alive. A doorman in a sharp, navy-blue-and-gold jacket spouted orders like a general and bellmen raced to follow them. Luxury cars idled beneath an arched stone covering over the gravel drive as guests stepped from them to be escorted into the hotel.

"This is…" she whispered, still stunned.

"I told you," Christian said. "Amazed."

"That's really not a big enough word," she told him as he pulled under the archway and stepped out of the car. In a moment, Christian was at the passenger side, helping her out. She stood up and did a slow turn, trying to take in everything at once.

It was impossible. She thought she'd need weeks to get the whole picture of the Jarrod resort. But what she had seen, she loved. Erica had never seen anyplace like it. It was as if she had stepped into a fairy tale. All that was missing was the handsome prince riding up on a black charger.

Then her gaze shifted to Christian. Handsome man in a black BMW. The modern version of the fairy tale then, she thought with an inner smile. But he wasn't a prince and she wasn't in need of rescuing. Or was she?

Shifting her gaze to scan the yard, then turning to peek through the open double doors into the lobby, Erica couldn't avoid a quick jolt of nerves that shot from her stomach up to her heart and back again. She was here. About to meet a family she'd never known and there was no going back.

"Second thoughts?"

She turned to look at Christian and found him watching her with a bemused expression on his face. Funny, she hadn't even met him a week ago and now, he was the one spot of familiarity in a rapidly changing world.

"No," she said firmly, taking a deep breath as she

did so. "No second thoughts. I made the decision to come here and I'm going to stick with it."

A flash of admiration lit up his dark eyes briefly and Erica felt warmed by it.

"Good for you," he said, then waved one arm out toward the interior of the hotel. "Ready to see your new home?"

"As I'll ever be," she told him and started walking.

The honey-colored wood walls and floors shone like a jewel box in the overhead lights. Framed photos of the mountain taken during every season dotted the walls and there were tables and chairs scattered around the wide lobby. A hum of conversation rose and fell as people wandered around the room and through it all, there was an almost electrical air about the place.

Erica swiveled her head from side to side, looking at everything as Christian guided her across the lobby to an elevator off by itself. "This is the private elevator to the family quarters," he told her and took a card from his pocket to slide into the key slot.

The door slid open and they stepped inside. Again, honey-colored wood set the tone, making Erica think not only of a mountain cabin, but warmth and luxury.

"Your key will be in your suite, waiting for you," Christian was saying. "Your luggage probably beat us here, since we took the scenic route. You'll find everything you need in your suite. There's even a small efficiency kitchen there and it's been stocked with the basics."

"Okay."

"There's also a main kitchen on the family level,

if you really feel the urge to cook something. But the hotel restaurants will deliver, so you don't have to worry about that if you don't want to."

"Oh, I like cooking," she told him as the elevator stopped and the door opened.

"Well, then, you and your brother Guy should get along just fine. He's a chef." Christian stepped out and held the door back for her. "He was, anyway. He owned his own restaurant in New York before coming back to Aspen and now he's pretty much taking over running the resort restaurants."

"A chef," she mused with a smile. "I'm not in his league, then. I said I like cooking. Didn't promise I was good at it."

"Make me dinner some night," he said, then stopped and frowned to himself as if he already regretted the words.

Judging by his expression, Erica ignored what he said, stepped into the hall and sighed as she looked around. "It just keeps getting prettier."

The hallway they stepped into was wide, leading off in two directions. Wood floors, walls the color of fog and a narrow table boasting a cobalt vase stuffed with roses and hydrangeas greeted her. Every few feet, an arched window let in sunlight and provided a view that was breathtaking. But she didn't have enough time to look around and enjoy it.

Christian pointed to the left. "Down there are four suites, and just past them, along the hallway, is the family room."

"Okay…" She noted that the private quarters

followed the line of the hotel, only the windows here looked out over a palatial pool area. The aquamarine water held a few guests lounging on rafts and on the flagstone area surrounding the pool, cabanas, tables and chairs with brightly colored umbrellas offered places to sit and chat. There was a bar tucked into one corner of the space and uniformed waiters and waitresses hurried back and forth seeing to the guests' comforts.

No doubt about it, she had walked into a very different world in Colorado than the one she was accustomed to. Then she realized that Christian was still talking and she turned around to watch him and listen.

"Past the family room is the original family quarters. The master bedroom and bedrooms for your brothers and sister when they were kids."

She tried to imagine growing up in this place, but it was hard to envision. So much space. So much open land for children to run and play. Smiling, she recalled that as a girl, she'd thought the park her nanny had taken her to was a veritable wilderness.

"As his kids got older," Christian said, "Don had the place rehabbed, building each of them their own suite and a few extras for guests."

It sounded as though Don Jarrod had done everything he could to keep his children at home. Yet each of them had fled Colorado. She had to wonder why.

Erica took a breath and nodded. "Are they all living here now?"

As if he could read the trepidation on her face, he smiled and said, "No. Right now, there's only Guy in one of the suites and Guy's twin, Blake, and his assistant living in two of the others. The rest of your family are here—staying in different lodges."

Only a couple of siblings to worry about facing every day then. That was good. Erica would prefer to settle in a little before she was forced to deal with Don Jarrod's other children. But if Guy or Blake and his assistant were there at the moment, now was as good a time as any to get the first of the introductions over with.

"Are any of them here now?" Erica tried to steel herself for meeting the first of her new family. Though now that she thought about it, she wished she had a minute to drag a brush through her wind-tossed hair and to put on some makeup and—

"No," Christian said, interrupting her frenzied thoughts. "Blake's gone for a few days at the moment. He and Samantha have been flying back and forth a lot to Vegas, wrapping up loose ends in the business and getting ready to take over here. Blake and your brother Gavin have been building hotels, mostly in Las Vegas and they've done exceptionally well out there."

"And they're giving it up to come back here?"

"Yeah," Christian said. "Like you, your brothers and sister have closed down their old lives and are here to start over again."

But they were returning to something familiar at least. She, on the other hand, felt as though she'd fallen into the rabbit hole. Nerves rattled through her again, but resolutely, she fought them down.

"What about Guy?"

"This time of day, he's probably downstairs in the main restaurant."

She drew a breath and let it go. "What about Gavin? Is he in Vegas with Blake?"

"No, he's here. But he's living in one of the private lodges on the grounds." Christian shrugged. "He wasn't interested in moving into the Manor."

Erica was beginning to understand that none of her brothers and sister were exactly thrilled to be back in Aspen. Yet, they'd all come, putting aside their plans and lives outside Jarrod Ridge to return and take up the family resort again. That told her that despite what were probably mixed feelings about their father and this place, their loyalty to family meant more than their reluctance to return. And that knowledge made her feel better, somehow. If family was everything to these people, then eventually, she might be able to have a relationship with all of them.

"What about the others?" she asked. "Where are they living?"

He led her down the hallway in the opposite direction from Blake's suite as he continued.

"Well, like I said, Trevor has his own place in Aspen, but he's here most days. Guy stays here mainly because he's working here at the Manor. And Melissa..." He paused. "She lives in Willow Lodge. It's the farthest lodge from the Manor, but anyone here can tell you where that is. She also runs the hotel spa, and you'll find her there most days."

"How big are the family quarters?" she suddenly

asked, astonished at the length of the hallway in both directions.

"As big as the top floor of the hotel. Including wings," Christian added with a smile.

"Amazing," she murmured as she followed after him.

"Yeah, it is. Down here is your suite, plus two more. Farther along this hall, you'll find the kitchen, the great room and what was Don's office. My office is down on the main floor, but I do most of my work at home."

"Right. You don't live at the Manor. Where's your place from here?"

He steered her toward one of the high, arched windows lining the hallway and pointed. "See the red roof just past that tall pine?"

She did. The building couldn't be more than a five-minute walk from where she was standing. "Close."

"It is. So if you ever need anything…"

He was standing so near, she felt heat radiating from his body toward hers. He smelled so good, she wanted to breathe deeper and when she looked up into those chocolate-brown eyes, she had the strangest desire to lean in and… *What* was she thinking? Didn't she have enough going on in her life at the moment?

"Thanks," she said abruptly, taking a safe step back from him. "I'll keep that in mind."

He watched her for a second or two and Erica wondered if he could tell what she'd been thinking. If he could see that she had been wondering what he would taste like. If his lips were as soft and warm as they appeared to be.

But if he did know, then he was as determined as she to not draw attention to it. He scrubbed one hand across his face, then waved one arm out in front of him in silent invitation to continue on down the hall. He walked beside her and the heels of their shoes sounded out like gunshots in the stillness.

When he finally stopped in front of a door and opened it, Erica stepped past him and stopped dead on the threshold.

It was gorgeous, which shouldn't have surprised her. Everything about Jarrod Ridge was breathtaking. But somehow, she hadn't expected her room to be so… wonderful. After all, she was the stranger here and from what she could tell so far, her new brothers and sister had been no more thrilled to hear of her existence than she had been to hear about them. She'd half expected an ordinary hotel room, lovely, but generic. This, she told herself as she walked farther into the room, was anything but generic.

The living room was done in various shades of blue. Pale blue walls, dark blue, overstuffed furniture, cobalt vases stuffed with flowers dripping heavy scent into the air and navy blue drapes at the arched windows. The wood floor was dotted with braided rugs in shades of blue and cream and even the fireplace was fronted by tiles that looked like delft.

"Wow," she said and even that word was just so insignificant to the task.

"Glad you like it," he said, moving into the room behind her.

"What's not to like?" She did a slow turn, trying

to see everything at once. Then her gaze landed on Christian again. "To tell the truth, I wasn't expecting anything like this."

He grinned briefly and something inside her twisted up tight in response. Really, the man had an almost magical smile. Good thing he didn't use it often.

"What were you expecting? A cell in a dungeon?"

She smiled and shrugged. "No, not that bad, but nothing so…"

"Melissa suggested you stay in this suite. She thought you'd like it and your brothers had no objection."

"No objection." Well, that was something, she supposed. "It was thoughtful of Melissa."

"You'll like her. She's looking forward to meeting you."

"And my brothers?"

He paused for a long moment before he said, "They'll come around."

"Just one big happy family, huh?" Funny, her excitement-driven nerves had become anxiety-driven in the blink of an eye. It seemed there were plenty of hard feelings for everyone to get through before they could even begin to relate to each other.

"You have as much right to be here as they do," he told her.

"Do I?" Erica shook her head and frowned as she threw out both hands as if to encompass the entire resort. "They grew up here. I'm the interloper. This is their *home*."

"The home that every one of them escaped from the minute they got the chance."

Her hands fell to her sides. "Why did they? Was Don Jarrod such a bad father?"

"Not bad," he said, crossing the room to stand by her side. "Just busy. Opinionated." Christian smiled ruefully. "He wasn't even my father and he was full of orders about what I should do with my life and the best way to do it."

"Sounds familiar," Erica mused, strolling to the window and staring out at the pool area and the mountains beyond. "I grew up with a father much like him. Ironic, isn't it?"

"Maybe that insight will make it easier for you to understand your siblings."

"I guess we'll see. Seems strange that this lovely place is practically empty. It's sad, somehow. That none of the Jarrods want to live in their family home."

"Well," Christian allowed, "like I told you, Don wasn't the easiest father in the world. Most of them have issues with the place and aren't very happy about the way their father arranged getting them back to Aspen."

She sighed a little. "So, we've got father troubles in common, anyway."

"You could say that." He shoved his hands into the back pockets of his jeans and watched her as she walked to the sofa in her new home. "Speaking of your father, how'd it go when you spoke with him about all of this?"

Erica shot him a look. "As I expected. He didn't want me to come."

"Why did you?"

She stopped, leaned over and picked up a throw pillow. She ran her fingertips across the heavily embroidered fabric, then set it down again. "I had to. I had to come and see and…"

"Find yourself?" he offered.

She laughed a little. "Sounds pompous, doesn't it?"

"Not really. I've been lost before. It's not always easy getting found again."

Erica tipped her head to one side and studied him. He looked so in control. So at home. So sure of himself, it was hard to imagine that he might have suffered self-doubt or anxiety. But she supposed everyone did from time to time. The trick was to not let those times get the best of you.

She turned around and let her gaze slide across the room that would be her home for who knew how long. There was a hallway off the living room that she assumed led to the bedroom and— "You said there was a stocked kitchen?"

"Yep." He pointed. "Right through there."

She went to investigate and off a short hall, she found a two-burner stove, a small refrigerator and several cupboards. The fridge was stocked with water, wine and soda along with fresh vegetables. There was a bowl of fruit on the abbreviated counter and she noticed that the window in the kitchen overlooked an English-style garden.

"You hungry?" Christian's voice came from directly behind her.

She turned around to look at him and admitted, "Actually, I am."

"Why don't we go get some lunch downstairs? I can answer your questions and you can meet one of your brothers at the same time."

That brother being Guy, she reminded herself. The chef. Well, that meeting just might kill her appetite, but gamely she said, "Give me one minute to freshen up and I'm ready."

Ready for all of it, she added silently.

Five

Guy Jarrod had once been a sought-after chef, with a reputation of excellence, but when he opened his own restaurant, he'd stepped out from behind the stove so to speak. He'd learned to love the business of running the restaurant even more than he had the actual art of cooking.

Now, he hired and fired chefs, made sure everything ran the way he wanted it to. But being back at Jarrod Ridge doing what he did best hadn't been on his agenda. Trust his father to make sure he eventually got his way where his children were concerned…even if it meant he had to die to do it.

Still irritated at being managed from beyond the grave, Guy had to admit that running the five-star restaurant at the Ridge was turning out to be a better gig than he'd expected it to be. He had big plans for the place.

Over the years, the restaurant and the general manager of the hotel had become, not lax, exactly, but complacent. They stayed with what worked rather than trying out new things. That was about to change.

All he had to do was get accustomed to being back here again.

"Excuse me, Mr. Jarrod?"

"What is it?" He looked up as one of the servers rushed into the wine cellar off the kitchen. A young kid who looked familiar, Guy hadn't had time to learn all their names yet.

"Mr. Hanford's in the dining room with a guest. He asked if you could come out to speak with them."

Christian. Well, part of being back in Aspen was going to entail dealing with his brothers, his sister— sisters, he reminded himself sternly—and Christian. They'd been friends once, Guy reminded himself. Now, they were business colleagues all because of one old man's stubborn refusal to let go of his children.

"Fine. Tell him I'll be right there." He left the wine cellar where he'd been taking a personal inventory—he wanted to know exactly what the restaurant had on hand and didn't trust anyone else to do it right.

That thought brought him up short. Maybe he was more like his old man than he'd ever thought.

He stalked through the kitchen, out into the main dining room, his gaze constantly shifting. He checked on the servers, on the table settings, on the flowers. He noticed the tablecloths and the flatware and the shine on the silver and brass espresso machine. He had a sharp eye, no tolerance for sloppy work and he intended to make good use of those traits now that he was back running this place the way it always should have been run.

Guy spotted Christian sitting at a booth in the back. As he got closer, he saw that across from him was a trim, pretty brunette with amber eyes. She looked vaguely familiar to him, but he couldn't place her. Which meant, Guy thought suddenly, *this* was the long-lost sister they'd all been waiting to meet. Her familiarity was simply that she had something of the Jarrod family stamped on her features.

They hadn't noticed his approach yet, so he took that spare moment to observe her. Pretty, he thought again. But she looked on edge. And hell, who could blame her? All of them had been dragged back to Jarrod Ridge whether they liked it or not.

Yet she had the worst of it, he thought. At least he and his siblings had each other. She was the stranger in a strange land. Despite a flicker of sympathy for her, though, Guy agreed with his twin. A newly acknowledged sister didn't deserve an equal share of the estate.

Christian caught Guy's gaze as the man approached. He also noticed the appraising gleam in the man's eyes as he gave Erica a quick once-over. He knew Erica was nervous about this meeting, but Christian was glad she would be starting out by meeting Guy. This Jarrod sibling had always had a cooler head than most of the others.

Well, except for Trevor. There wasn't much in life that shook Trevor.

"Christian, good to see you," Guy said, but he wasn't looking at him. Instead the man's eyes were locked on Erica. "And you must be my new little sister."

She flushed nervously, but she lifted her chin, stuck out her hand and said, "That's me. But I usually go by Erica."

"Good one," he said and shook her hand briefly. "So, you getting settled in?"

"I am, but I think it's going to take me a while to be able to find my way around."

"I'm pretty sure the front desk has maps," he said, giving her a smile. "What do you think of the Manor?"

"It's gorgeous," she blurted, looking around the half-full dining room at the guests gathered there. "It must have been a wonderful place to grow up."

"You'd think so, wouldn't you?" Guy tugged at the edge of the tablecloth, smoothing out a tiny wrinkle in the fine linen. "Christian told us you were in PR back in San Francisco."

"Yes, I was."

"That'll come in handy, then." A server slipped up behind him, whispered something and then drifted away again. "I'm sorry. There's something in the kitchen I need to handle. Christian, good to see you again. Erica…" He shifted his gaze to hers and held it for a long moment before smiling. "I'll be seeing you around."

When he was gone, Erica blew out a breath.

"Wasn't so bad, was it?" Christian watched her as she reached for her water glass and took a sip. Guy could have been a little more welcoming, but on a scale of one to ten, ten being a warm hug and one a shotgun reception—he'd scored about a five.

"A little nerve-racking, but all in all, not bad," she admitted. Then she asked, "What did Guy mean, my PR skill will come in handy?"

Christian had wanted to give her a day or two to get used to being here, but there was no point in putting things off. There was a lot coming up and since she was now expected to take her place in the Jarrod family, she might as well get her feet wet right away.

"The food and wine gala is coming up in a few weeks," he said. "It's a big deal in Aspen. Held every year, lasts several weeks and has foodie and wine lovers in the country and in Europe coming into town to enjoy themselves."

"I've read about it," she said. "And seen some coverage on the news every year, too. It's practically a Mardi Gras type thing, isn't it?"

"Close enough," he told her. "The city depends on the tourism dollars and the gala the Jarrods sponsor is a big part of that. As one of the Jarrods, you're right in the middle of this one."

Her eyes went wide, but she nodded and said, "Tell me."

Again, he had to admire how she was able to go with

the flow. She was strong, but she had the tendency to bend, not break. Most of the women he'd known in his life would still be sitting in San Francisco trying to come to terms with everything she'd dealt with in the last few days. Not Erica Prentice though. Once her decision was made, she gave it her all.

For a tiny thing, she was formidable.

Her gaze was locked on him and he found himself getting distracted by those amber depths. By the way she chewed at her bottom lip when she was thinking. Hell, he was distracted by her, period.

Grumbling to himself, his voice was brusque and businesslike as he said, "Your brother Trevor is the marketing expert. He's been running his own company right here in Aspen for years. Now, he's taking over the marketing for Jarrod Ridge."

"Big job."

"It is," he said, "and so is yours. You'll be the new head of the Ridge's PR department."

When she looked startled, he added, "You'll be working with Trevor directly on most of it. You'll have your own office at the Manor, so you'll be on site more often than Trevor. The two of you will probably see a lot of each other over the next few weeks."

"Won't that be fun."

Worry had crept into her voice again and he reminded her, "Trevor's pretty laid-back. He's not going to be a hard-ass, so nothing to worry about there."

She took a deep breath. "Hope you're right about that."

"I am. Just as I'm right about thinking you'll handle yourself well here."

"Right into the deep end then?"

"Any reason to think you can't swim?" Christian asked and watched as she seemed to consider his question.

Finally, she shook her head, gave him a fierce, bright smile and said, "I'll swim."

"I bet you will," he said, staring at her as she picked up her leather-backed menu and perused the offerings. He wished to hell he didn't find her more and more intriguing with every passing minute. What was it about this one small, curvy woman that had his body tied up in knots and his brain overheating?

Was it the lure of the unattainable?

He didn't think so. There had been plenty of women when he was younger who had been out of his league. A townie kid with a single mom didn't really have the means to play in the ball games of the rich and famous. But he wasn't that kid anymore and he could have the pick of any woman he wanted.

What he couldn't figure out was why that didn't seem to matter.

The one woman he wanted was also the one woman he couldn't have.

Two hours later, Erica was alone in her suite. Sunset was deepening into twilight but here in her rooms, the lamplight was bright and she was too wrapped up in what she was doing to even notice the end of her first day in Colorado. Christian had gone back to work after their early meal—excusing himself as quickly as possible with a claim of having to get some work done before morning. Once she was on her own, Erica had done a little exploring.

Now, she sat on the couch in her new living room and looked at all of the magazines, books, postcards and brochures she had spread out around her. She'd practically bought out the gift shop downstairs, buying up every item she could find pertaining directly to Jarrod Ridge.

And there had been plenty to choose from. The brochures listed every activity to be found at the resort and the book described the history of the place. She'd stared at the black-and-white photos of her grandparents and biological father with a fascination that had kept her captive for nearly twenty minutes. The grainy images of men in worn jeans and cowboy hats were so far removed from the tidy heritage she'd grown up hearing about, it was fascinating. She'd looked for resemblances between the people in those old pictures and herself and she'd found them. The shape of her eyes, the curve of her mouth. It was odd to see something of herself in people she had never met.

Yet in a weird way, it was almost comforting.

Her family was bigger than she'd ever imagined. They had been adventurers, dreamers. Men and women who had come to the middle of nowhere and built a life, a legacy that had lasted. Their dreams had grown and blossomed and had become something very special.

And she was a part of it.

A very small link in a lengthy chain.

When a knock sounded on her door, she was at first surprised, then a second later, a little worried about who might be dropping by. But then, she thought, it might be Christian. He might have decided to come back and take her on a little tour of the hotel. That thought spurred her off the couch and toward the front door. She fluffed her hair, smoothed her shirt and smiled to herself at the prospect of being with him again.

But when she opened the door, there was a woman standing there, holding two bottles of wine.

"Red or white?" she asked, walking past Erica into the living room.

"I'm sorry?" Confused, Erica just watched her.

"Red or white? Which do you prefer?"

"Uh, that depends, I guess…"

The woman grinned at her. "Good answer. I'm your sister, Melissa. And I've just stolen some wine from our brother Guy's private reserve so that you and I can get to know each other."

Hard to feel out of sorts or uncomfortable with Melissa Jarrod beaming goodwill toward her. Although the woman did manage to make Erica feel a little frumpy in her wrinkled clothes. Melissa was wearing sleek black jeans, an off the shoulder, silk turquoise top and black sandals that were really nothing more than three slinky straps and a three-inch heel. Her long blond hair hung loose down her back and her wide blue eyes were sparkling with challenge and welcome.

"You stole the wine from Guy?" Erica repeated, closing the door, then turning to face her sister.

"Sure did. There may be hell to pay tomorrow, but tonight, we party."

"That actually sounds like a great plan," Erica said, smiling.

Melissa grinned right back. "Just so you know," she said, "if we both drink it, we both face Guy's wrath. A united sister front."

"Sisters," Erica repeated.

Melissa wrinkled her nose then shrugged. "I know. Sounds weird still, doesn't it? Does to me, too. But I think you and I are going to make a terrific team."

Erica felt a bit of her earlier tension slide off her shoulders. Looking into her sister's eyes, knowing that this welcome was genuine, made her feel that maybe making a home at Jarrod Ridge wasn't going to be as difficult as she had thought it would be.

"You know," Erica said, "I think you're right. So, do you know if they stocked wineglasses in my new kitchen?"

Melissa led the way and threw back over her shoulder, "Since I'm the one who ordered the stocking done, I happen to know that wineglasses were first on the list."

"Excellent," Erica said following her into the tiny kitchen. "I'll make some popcorn, so let's start with the white. What do you think?"

Melissa set both bottles down onto the counter, then turned and held out her hand to Erica. "It's a good choice. Guy stocks the best sauvignon blanc anywhere in Colorado."

"And how will he feel about us helping ourselves?"

Erica asked as she took Melissa's outstretched hand in hers for a shake.

Shrugging, Melissa said, "Guess we'll find out. Together?"

"Together," Erica agreed and for the first time since she'd arrived in Colorado, felt that there was a real chance she would be able to make her own place there.

Then the two women moved companionably in the small kitchen, getting to know each other as they worked. Halfway through the second bottle of wine—they'd decided to open another bottle of white that had been stocked in Erica's fridge—the two women were well on their way to being fast friends.

"You make excellent popcorn," Melissa announced.

"Thank you. I told Christian I could cook."

"And was he impressed?" Melissa shook her head. "No, never mind. Probably not. The only things that impresses Christian are ledgers, files and injunctions."

"You've known him a long time?" Erica asked, settling back into the couch and curling her feet up beneath her.

Melissa was tucked into the opposite corner of the couch. "Forever," she said. "Since we were kids. Of course, back then, Christian was working for the resort and dear old dad didn't approve of family and employees hanging out together. But I saw him all the time and the boys and he were sort of friends even back then. When Christian was a teenager, my father took an interest in him." She frowned, took a sip of wine and said, "Dad loved to point out that Christian didn't have any of the advantages that *we* had and yet his drive to succeed eclipsed ours." Shaking her head at the memory, she said, "Let me tell you, there was a lot of irritation toward the great Christian when we were kids. Dad dangled his accomplishments in front of us like a perpetual taunt." Melissa shook her head in memory. "Good thing Christian was such a nice guy or things might've gotten ugly. Anyway, my point is, once Dad noticed him, Christian was around the Manor a lot more."

Erica's mind drew up a picture of a young Christian, battling for success, trying to find a place for himself amidst the Jarrod family. It seemed she and he had a lot in common. Here she was, after all, trying to do the same thing that he had so many years ago. But it wasn't only his adapting into the Jarrod world she was curious about. She wondered what his life had been like before Don Jarrod. In fact, she just wondered about Christian in general. Thoughts of him were never far from her mind, even though she told herself that now was definitely not the time to indulge in an attraction. She had to find her own footing here. Did she really have time to explore a relationship? And did she dare risk trusting someone so new in her life? Besides, it wasn't as if Christian had made a move. Maybe she was alone in feeling the draw toward him. And if she was, then she'd keep it to herself.

"So," she said, "your father took an interest in Christian and then what?"

"*Our* father," Melissa corrected with a brief smile. "He helped him get into college, then hired him when he got out of law school. He's worked for the Ridge most of his life, I guess. Dad made up his mind that Christian was going to be the official Jarrod Ridge attorney and that was that. Our father wasn't someone easy to walk away from." Then she cocked her head to one side. "Hearing me call him *our* father must be very strange for you."

"It is." Erica thought that was the biggest understatement of all time. She had hardly had time to wrap her own mind around it. Now finding herself sitting here with her *sister* was just one more oddity in a world suddenly turned upside down. But despite the craziness, she liked the camaraderie that Melissa had instigated. "Though you're making it easier."

"Happy to help. Trust me, I'm glad to have another female in the Jarrod ranks."

"Thanks," Erica said and meant it. In all the strangeness of her new world, it was good to have at least one person here who seemed to be on her side. Why Melissa had decided to be an ally seemed clear enough. Heaven knew that Erica would have loved to have a sister to help her stand against her older brothers occasionally.

"Now," Melissa asked, pointing at the piles of brochures and pamphlets scattered across the coffee table, "what are you doing with all of this stuff?"

Laughing, Erica scooped up one or two of the forgotten pamphlets. "I was trying to learn all I could about Jarrod Ridge."

Melissa took a sip of wine. "There's an easier way. Just ask me."

"Okay, I will as soon as I figure out what to ask."

"Deal. So, Christian told me you're in PR?"

Glad for a respite of talking about her now tangled family ties, Erica said, "Yes, and apparently that's what I'll be doing here, too."

"That means working with Trevor. You'll like him. Easygoing, hard to ruffle," Melissa said, "unlike the rest of the bunch."

"I met Guy this afternoon."

"How'd that go?"

"Cool, but polite."

"That sounds about right," Melissa told her. "Of the twins, Guy's more reasonable. Blake not so much. But he'll come around. Just don't let him scare you off."

That didn't sound promising, Erica thought, now even more reluctant than ever to meet Blake Jarrod. But there would be no way to avoid it and now, knowing for sure that he was going to be less than welcoming, it gave her a chance to prepare. To be ready to stand up for herself as she'd had to do most of her life.

"I'm here and I'm not leaving," Erica told her. "If Blake's unhappy with that, he'll just have to get over it."

"Good for you!" Melissa grinned at her, obviously pleased at her new sister's inner strength.

If only she knew, Erica thought, that right now, her strength was little more than a carefully constructed front. Inside, she was quavering. But she, too, would get over it.

"Now then," Melissa was saying, "there's Gavin to deal with, too. He's sort of shut-off emotionally, so probably won't be much trouble. But good luck getting a smile out of him."

"He sounds a lot like my older brothers."

"That's right. Christian told me that you're the only girl in your family, too. What do your brothers think of you being here?"

"They tried to talk me out of it—as did my fa—" she caught herself and amended what she had been going to say. "Walter."

Melissa reached out and patted her hand, sending her a commiserating smile at the same time. "It's going to get confusing with all of the fathers around here, isn't it?"

"I suppose."

"Look, my dad may have been your biological father, but Walter's still the man who raised you," Melissa said softly.

"I know, it's just…" How to explain her need to stand alone, to find answers? To live with the feelings of guilt and betrayal she had for turning her back on Walter, despite the fact that she'd never really felt any real warmth from him?

"So, are you and Walter close?"

"No," she answered quietly, wishing she could say otherwise. "How about you and your dad?"

Melissa sighed and shook her head. "No. I was two when my mother died and my father didn't really know what to do with me, I guess. So he did nothing." She smiled ruefully. "I know how it sounds, poor little rich girl. The truth is though, Erica, you got the better end of this bargain. You weren't raised here."

"At least you had this place," Erica told her. "It's so beautiful here."

"A golden jail is still a cell." A long moment of silence passed during which Erica didn't have a clue what to say or do. She'd have liked to offer her sister comfort, but wasn't at all sure it would be welcome. Besides, she knew all too well that sympathy didn't always salve ancient hurts. Sometimes it only made it worse. So she kept quiet and waited until Melissa came out of her musings herself.

"Anyway, ancient history for both of us, right? Moving on. So, PR girl…what do you think about helping me design a new menu of services for the spa?" She grabbed the old one off the coffee table and glared at it. "This one is so generic it's tired. I'd like something splashy. Something bright. Oh, and something about the yoga classes I'm going to be teaching. Do you do yoga?"

Erica laughed at the rapid-fire statements, grateful that they'd left the subject of their fathers and sad, lonely childhoods behind. Shaking her head, she said, "Yoga? No thanks. I'm just not that bendy. But I'd love to work up a new brochure with you. If I have time with the food and wine gala preparations…"

"Oh, yeah." Melissa sighed in disgust. "True. Okay, once you get that going, then we'll tend to my little slice of Jarrod Ridge."

"Sounds good."

"So," Melissa said, and lifted her wineglass in a toast. "Here's to us. Sisters by birth, friends by choice."

"Here's to us," Erica said and clinked her glass against the rim of Melissa's. She could only hope that the remaining meetings with her siblings would go even half so well.

Six

The next morning, Gavin walked into the Manor to meet Erica Prentice in Christian's office.

Sister?

Not as far as he was concerned. She was a stranger who shared a little Jarrod DNA. Logically, he knew that she, too, was being manipulated from the grave by Don Jarrod. But it didn't make her being here all right.

He wasn't sure how he felt about this new sister taking up a place at Jarrod Ridge. Hell, he wasn't even happy about having to be there himself. But for him it was different. The Manor was filled with memories, good and bad. He felt his father's presence everywhere in the old building and knew that wherever Don was now, the old man was enjoying watching his children wrestle with the terms of his will.

"Just like him," Gavin muttered as he walked through the crowded lobby, discounting the low roar of dozens of voices locked in conversations. He continued on along the hall toward Christian's office, resenting the fact that he was here at all. He'd made a life apart from the Ridge and his father had known it. But then, he thought, that would have been half the fun for Don. Upsetting his children's plans to ensure that his own worked out as he wanted.

"Nothing Don liked better than stirring things up and seems like he's done a great job of it this time," he told himself.

He'd already talked to Guy and Melissa about their new sister and while Guy was withholding judgment, Melissa had, of course, come down on Erica's side. Though he appreciated the input, Gavin would make up his own mind and he believed firmly in not putting off what could get done today.

Unlike Blake. He knew damn well that Blake had left for Vegas deliberately this time, not wanting to be at the Manor when Erica arrived. As for Trevor, well, he was supposed to be here this morning but he'd do whatever felt right for him at the moment.

As if his thoughts had conjured him out of thin air, Gavin's youngest brother pushed away from a wall and lifted one hand in greeting.

"Wasn't sure you'd come in," Trevor said.

"I told you I'd be here."

Trevor smiled. "And you're always exactly where you're expected to be."

"There something wrong with that?"

"No," Trevor answered with a shake of his head, "But don't you ever get tired of leading such a regimented life?"

"It's not—" He broke off, clearly not interested in rehashing the same old discussion.

Trevor admired his oldest brother. Hell, as a kid, he'd practically worshipped him. But now that they were all grown, Trevor thought Gavin's life could use some shaking up. Coming back to the Ridge was a start, but he needed more. The man was wound too tight, Trevor told himself sadly. While he, on the other hand, took life as it came, did as he wanted and planned to have no regrets when it came time for him to check out.

Just another reason he'd gone along with his late father's machinations to get them all back to the Ridge. Not that Trevor had gone far from the Jarrod family home. And why would he have? He loved skiing and he'd never find better than what Aspen could offer. Besides, he had his house in town, his own company and too many friends to just pack up and disappear.

So he'd stayed in Colorado while everyone else had gone. He'd missed his brothers and sister, though, so despite how it had happened, he was glad they'd come back.

As for his new sister, Trevor was willing to give her a shot. After all, it wasn't her fault Don Jarrod was her father.

"So, you ready to meet her?" Gavin asked.

Trevor snorted a laugh. "You don't have to make it sound like we're going to a hanging."

His brother sighed. "And you don't have to turn it into a social event."

"It *is* a social event, man. We're going to meet our long-lost sister and unless you're trying to scare her off, you might want to paste a smile on your face."

"You smile enough for both of us."

"You're hopeless, you know that, right?" Trevor asked and then, more seriously, said, "She's probably more upset by all this than we are, Gavin. Maybe you could cut her a little slack?"

"Fine. Slack for the newcomer. No slack for you."

Trevor laughed.

Grumbling, Gavin fell into step alongside his brother and swung past the hotel's business center. They walked on to Christian's office. The man didn't have a secretary guarding his gate. Instead, he used the employees of the business center to take care of whatever tasks he needed done. Which made dropping in on him even easier.

After a brisk knock, Gavin opened the door and stepped inside, with Trevor just a pace behind him.

Looking up from his paperwork, Christian smiled. "She's not here yet."

"Late, huh?" Gavin pointed out.

"No," Trevor corrected with a sigh and shake of his head. "We're early." Then he walked into the room and dropped into one of the available chairs. Looking at Christian he asked, "So what's the newest Jarrod like?"

Christian leaned back in his chair and studied the two men. Gavin was standing off to one side, his arms folded across his chest. Trevor, on the other hand, looked the picture of relaxation. The two of them had offered to come in to meet Erica together and Christian had agreed, hoping Trevor's presence would be enough to mitigate Gavin's penchant for aloofness.

"What's she like?" he mused, and instantly his mind filled with images of Erica. Her eyes, her mouth, her delicate, but curvy figure and just how much he wanted her. But an instant later, he shut those thoughts down as quickly as he could. Not exactly the description he could give Erica's brothers.

"She's smart. Funny. Strong." His gaze shifted from Gavin to Trevor and back again. "She's nervous, as anyone would be, but she's determined to make this a success."

"Why is this so important to her?" Gavin asked.

"Hate to admit it, but good question," Trevor agreed.

Frowning, Christian said, "You know what your relationship with Don was like. Well, that's what she had with the man who raised her. From what I can gather, she was cut out of their family business and now that she's been brought into this one, she's focused on making it work."

"Focused."

Christian looked at Gavin. "She knows that you guys aren't exactly ready to throw her a welcome-to-the-family party. And from what I can gather, she's used to that kind of behavior from her older brothers."

"Well, that's telling us," Trevor muttered. "So we

can play nice or we can be the bastard brothers she's accustomed to."

"Exactly," Christian said with a nod. It was important to him that they understand. That they give Erica the chance she deserved. He wasn't willing to explore *why* it was important to him, though. Point was, "She's innocent in this, you know. If you're pissed that your father had an affair with her mother, be pissed at *him*."

Gavin shifted position uneasily as if he were feeling the stirrings of guilt and didn't like it a damn bit. "I didn't say I blamed her for any of this. It's just a difficult situation. For everyone."

"It is," Erica said softly.

Christian's gaze snapped to the doorway and the woman who stood poised, alone, watching them. He stood up and said, "Erica."

She spared him a quick smile, but it was gone too soon in Christian's opinion. What was it about this woman that grabbed at him? Why was he having so much trouble reminding himself that as an employee of Jarrod Ridge, the Jarrod family was off-limits to him?

Trevor came lazily to his feet and Gavin turned to face their younger sister.

"I didn't mean to interrupt," she was saying as she walked into the room, with her chin tilted defiantly. "But I couldn't help overhearing. Since I was the topic of conversation anyway, I thought it was as good a time as any to introduce myself."

Christian spared brief glances at both of the Jarrod

men and he saw Gavin trying to think back and figure out if he'd said anything he should apologize for. While, at the same time, Trevor's mouth was quirked in an approving smile.

"Erica," Christian said, coming around his desk to align himself at her side—both physically and figuratively. "These are your brothers, Gavin and Trevor."

She returned Trevor's smile, then looked at Gavin. They stared at each other for a long minute and Christian could actually feel the tension building in the room. And then suddenly, it was gone as Gavin stepped forward, held out his hand to her and said, "Welcome, Erica."

She only hesitated an instant before shaking his hand. "Thank you. I heard you say this was difficult and you're not wrong. This whole situation has been just as hard on me as it has been on all of you."

"You're right," Trevor said as he came up to join them. "And whatever you heard before you came in, pay no attention. Everybody's a little on edge, being back at the Ridge, and that's bleeding over into everything else."

"I appreciate that," she told him.

Christian felt that stir of admiration for her again for how well she stood up to brothers who clearly weren't eager to have her in the family. Whether she was wanted to be here or not, she had a place at the Ridge. Through birth. Through blood. Because Don Jarrod had wanted to bring *all* of his children home.

"Once you're settled in, come and see me," Trevor

was saying. "We've got the food and wine gala right around the corner now. Most of the marketing and publicity is already lined up and in play. But there are a few things we can still do to give it that final push."

Erica nodded. "I've heard about the gala for years, though I've never attended. I'm looking forward to being a part of it this year. Last night, Melissa showed me some of what you'd been doing and it's really fabulous."

He grinned, apparently satisfied.

"But," she added, "I've got a few ideas we might want to try."

His eyes narrowed on her thoughtfully, then after a moment, he gave her a grin. "I like confidence, so yeah, I'd like to hear your ideas. Tomorrow work for you?"

"Tomorrow's great."

Gavin interrupted them. "I know this isn't easy on you, being here. Being thrown into the middle of something you didn't even know existed a week ago."

"No," she said, "it's not."

He nodded. "I came in here prepared to not like you," he admitted and smiled when she stiffened. "But I've got a lot of respect for anybody who's not afraid to stand up for him—or herself."

"And I respect anyone who's trying to protect his family," Erica told him. "As for standing up for myself, I've been doing that my whole life."

"I'm getting that," Gavin said with an approving nod. "I think you just might make a place for yourself here…little sister."

Erica gave him a careful smile, pleased but clearly

not willing to relax her guard just yet. Then the moment was over and the Jarrod brothers were excusing themselves.

Christian couldn't take his eyes off of her. He hardly noticed when his friends left. All he saw were two amber-colored eyes watching him with a mixture of nervousness and satisfaction shining in their depths. She was pleased with the way she'd handled herself and damned if he wasn't, as well.

He'd set this meeting up specifically so that he would be there when she met her brothers. So that she wouldn't be alone. Not that he didn't believe the Jarrod siblings, even if they were angry about the situation, would be anything but polite. It was only that Christian had wanted her to have his support and *know* that she had it. He didn't ask himself why that was important to him, he only accepted that it was.

She was still nervous, but the others wouldn't have been able to tell. Funny, but he'd once thought her features easy to read. Now he knew the truth. Though she might be quaking in her shoes, she'd never let anyone know it.

Their first meeting had been different. She'd been taken off guard and her shock and stunned surprise had been impossible to hide. But he'd learned since that the only real hint to what Erica Prentice was feeling lay in her eyes. There, her emotions shone out loud and clear.

Despite her lifted chin and firm voice, those eyes of hers showed him that she was silently battling her own fears. Yet despite everything, every time she went into battle, she came out victorious. He admired the hell out of that. Almost as much as he wanted her.

Desire was now a constant companion. Haunting him through his sleep, torturing him during the day. Thoughts of her were never far away and his body was in a constant state of arousal. He'd never before felt such a powerful pull toward any woman. And every moment he spent with her only intensified those feelings.

"Gee, that went well," she said after a moment or two of silence that practically throbbed with unresolved tension.

"Believe it or not, it did," Christian answered. "I think you impressed both of them."

Her gaze fixed on his. "I wasn't trying to impress."

"Maybe that's why you did. Just by being yourself. They respect strength."

She smiled ruefully. "Good thing they couldn't hear my knees knocking then, isn't it?" She walked across his office and looked out the window behind his desk at the sweep of lawn that seemed to stretch all the way to the mountains. "You arranged that meeting specifically so I wouldn't stumble across my...brothers on my own, didn't you?"

"Yeah," he admitted. "I thought it would be easier if I were around."

She turned her head to look directly at him. Her gaze slammed into his. "It was. Thank you."

He stared into her eyes and it was all he could do to keep from going to her, sweeping her into his arms and kissing her until neither of them could breathe. But somehow he managed. "You're welcome. You've still got Blake to meet and deal with, but he should be back in a couple of days."

"From what everyone says, I'm not looking forward to meeting him."

"Blake's all right," Christian told her, not wanting her to be anxious over the last Jarrod hurdle she had to face. "He's not really happy with the situation, but he knows none of this is your fault."

She blew out a breath. "What do you think, Christian? You're the objective observer in all this. Do you think this is going to work out?"

"You being here, you mean?" When she nodded, he walked closer to her. "Yes, I do. You're already making a place for yourself here. Your sister likes you. Your brothers will come around."

Erica shook her head and her light brown hair lifted from her shoulders, then fell back again in soft waves. Christian curled his hands into fists to keep from reaching for it. To keep from threading his fingers through that mass and turning her head toward his—

"Why are you on my side in this?" Erica asked. "Melissa says you've known the family since you were a kid. And you were Don's personal attorney. I'd think that would make you more prejudiced in their favor rather than mine."

He backed up a step, leaned against the corner of his desk and said, "Don Jarrod was a hard man to know. He helped me when I was a teenager. Offered me a job here when I got out of law school. But," he added, "that said, I don't owe him or his memory my soul. Just the best job I can do. My allegiances are my own."

She tipped her head to one side and looked up at him. "And you've decided to be my ally."

"Yeah."

"Why?"

"Do you really have to ask?"

"Shouldn't I?"

He shrugged, though it cost him. He wanted her to trust him, but couldn't say that he trusted himself around her. He wanted more than friendship or an alliance with her. But if he took more, he'd risk everything he'd already built.

"Let's just say that whatever I owe the Jarrods, I owe myself more. So I'm on your side because I've had a hand in throwing your life off kilter."

"So you feel responsible? You don't have to," she told him. "Like I said earlier, I can take care of myself."

"I've noticed," he said, then forced a smile. "Let's get out of here. How about a tour of the grounds?"

"I'd like that," she said and took the arm he offered before walking with him out of the office and the hotel.

They walked for what felt like miles.

Erica was overwhelmed with everything. She was on sensory overload. Jarrod Ridge had to be the most beautiful place she'd ever been and it was staggering to realize that she was a part of the legacy that had built it.

The resort was like a small town in and of itself.

Narrow walkways, cement pathways bordered by vibrant flower beds, wound past tiny bungalows and lavish cabins. Christian had stopped by his own home to give her a quick tour and Erica had loved everything about it. From the honey-colored log walls to the braided rugs on the polished wood floors to the overstuffed, brown leather furniture.

He had a river stone fireplace big enough to stand up in and the huge windows in his kitchen overlooked the forest and the mountain beyond. She could imagine stepping out onto the back porch, sitting in one of the rocking chairs there and sipping a morning cup of coffee as she watched the world wake up.

Seeing his home had given her more insights into Christian the man and she relished them. He was neat, but not to the point of craziness. He had actual pots and pans in his kitchen, which meant he at least tried to cook occasionally rather than subsisting on room service or takeout. He had framed family photos hanging on his wall and seeing him as a younger man with one arm thrown across his mother's shoulders told her that he was someone to whom family meant a lot. All good things. And all of those things combined made him even more intriguing to Erica.

When they left his house, Erica was more captivated by him than she had been before. She took his arm as he led her on through the resort. He pointed out the cabins where Gavin and Melissa lived. He'd shown her the gift shops, the jewelers, the on-site bakery and the ice cream parlor. He'd taken her past the pools—both the indoor and outdoor, not to mention the pool built just for kids.

Guests in swimsuits, tennis gear and even riding outfits streamed over the property in a never-ending flood of humanity. Children raced each other across manicured lawns and a couple of elderly guests sat on a padded iron bench beneath a gorgeous cluster of aspen trees.

The sun was out, the sky was blue and she honestly felt as though she'd stepped into an alternate world. Everything was almost too perfect.

Including the man at her side. He wasn't wearing a suit and tie, just black jeans, a white, long-sleeved shirt open at the throat and a pair of black boots that looked as though they had seen a lot of wear. He looked handsome in a well-cut suit, but Erica thought he looked even more so in casual clothes. It was then a person realized that his personal power wasn't shaped by any outward appearance—not his clothing, his car or his job—but by his own innate strength.

And that, Erica thought, was about the sexiest thing in the world.

She loved how people knew him. Smiled, waved, stopped to speak to him as they walked. He introduced her to managers and housemaids, all with respect and deference. He treated everyone the same and she found that sexy as hell, too. She'd been raised by a man who believed in the perception of status. Walter would never have introduced a friend of his to a maid—but Christian was a different sort of man. The kind she'd been looking for before her life turned upside down.

Now, she had to wonder if part of her attraction for him wasn't because he was the only familiar face around her. But no, even as she considered that, she put it aside. There was much more to what she was feeling for Christian Hanford.

"So what do you think?"

She looked up at him and loved how the wind had ruffled his short dark hair onto his forehead. She just managed to catch herself from reaching up and pushing it back. "Um," she said, gathering up her scattered thoughts, "I hate to keep using the word *amazing....*"

He grinned, and her breath locked in her lungs. Seriously, when the man flashed an unguarded smile, he was a danger to any woman with eyes.

He pointed off in the distance. "The stables are down there, alongside a paddock, and there are riding trails through the woods. Tennis courts are over there and the golf course is back at the opposite end of the resort."

She laughed to herself. "It's like a little city all in itself."

"Exactly how Don saw it, too," Christian said. "We've even got a small clinic on site. Joel Remy runs it. He's got a nurse who helps out and they can take care of any minor situations the guests might have. Of course, anything more serious is treated at the hospital in Aspen."

"Our own medical staff. Wow." She turned from him and stared out at the surrounding cabins and lodges.

"That's the first time you've said 'our' about this place," he commented. "Starting to feel more connected?"

She looked back at him. "I guess I am. It's a little nerve-racking, but I'm excited about it, too, you know?"

"I do," he said, then looked around as she had, as if he were seeing it for the first time through her eyes. Finally, he turned his gaze back on her. "You'll make your place here, Erica."

"Yeah," she said, giving him a smile that lit up her eyes. "I will."

He nodded as if he sensed her commitment, and said, "A long time ago, I decided to make this my place. To carve out my own slice of Jarrod Ridge."

"Why? I mean, what drove you to want this?" She asked the question quietly, not wanting to disturb the intimacy of the moment. Despite the fact that they were surrounded on all sides by happy, chattering guests, it felt as though they were alone, just the two of them.

He smiled to himself and tucked his hands into his jeans pockets. "I told you I grew up here. Well, in Aspen."

She nodded but didn't say anything, encouraging him silently to continue.

"My first job was as a busboy in the main restaurant in the Manor." He glanced back over his shoulder at the palatial mansion, its rose brick walls nearly radiant in the bold, summer sunshine. "I loved it. Well, not working in the restaurant, but being here. Being a part of it all." He paused, as though he were gathering up stray thoughts and straightening them out. "My dad died when I was three. My mom worked constantly, but it was hard, you know?"

Erica nodded, caught up in the soft cadence of his words, the faraway look in his eyes.

"Anyway…" He took a long breath and released it again. "I knew what I wanted. I wanted to belong at a place like this. So I worked my ass off in school, got a scholarship and eventually, with Don's help, went to law school."

"Why did he help?" she asked, curious now about the father she would never know.

"To tell you the truth, I don't really know," he admitted with a half smile. "There was never any telling what Don would do or why. I like to think he saw something in me he thought would work well here. That he knew I'd do the job for him."

"Sounds like that's exactly what he thought," she told him.

Christian sent her a glance. "Maybe. I'll never know for sure. I do know that he helped shape me into the kind of lawyer I am. And I helped him reshape this place into the growth it's enjoying now."

"Then you did what you set out to do," Erica said. "Made a place for yourself. Ensured that you belong here."

"Yeah, I did. And I owed Don a lot—which," he added wryly, "he never let me forget."

"What's that mean?" It didn't sound good and by the look on his face, Christian wasn't happy about whatever he was going to tell her.

"It means, that in my contract with the resort, Don laid it out just the way he wanted it. Hell, he even made sure the codicil was in his will, just in case I needed reminding."

"What?" A curl of apprehension settled in the pit of her stomach. Erica had the distinct feeling she wasn't going to like what he was about to say.

Christian locked his gaze with hers. "For me to keep my invested shares in Jarrod Ridge, I'm to remain loyal to the business."

"That doesn't sound so bad."

"Then there's the added warning to stay away from his daughters."

"What?" Erica shook her head as if she hadn't heard him right. "Say that again."

Christian huffed out a breath. "He didn't put it in those words, exactly, but the meaning's clear enough. I might be a big-time, rich lawyer now, but Don still saw me as the poor kid looking for a chance. And he didn't want that kid anywhere near his daughters. Either of them. Bottom line, Erica? You're off-limits."

Seven

"But that's ridiculous," Erica argued, astounded at this turn of events.

He shrugged. "That's Don."

"It's medieval." She took a step away from him, turned around and came right back. Looking up into his chocolate eyes, Erica felt that bone-deep hum she always did when she was around him. She knew he felt it, too. She could see desire in his eyes, feel heat rippling off him in thick waves. Erica looked up at him. "Why are you telling me this?"

"You know why," he said and his eyes darkened even as his mouth tightened into a hard line. "Because there's something between us."

"So you want to stop it."

"Didn't say I wanted to," he corrected with a shake

of his head. "But this is my life. One I worked damn hard for."

"That's right," she countered. "*Your* life. And *mine*. Don Jarrod has nothing to do with this."

He snorted a laugh. "The fact that you can say that and mean it just goes to prove you didn't know him."

"No, I didn't. But even if I had, I wouldn't let him make my decisions for me," she snapped. Anger shot through her and she let her words ride the wave of it. "I didn't let Walter decide whether I'd move here or not. I won't let Don decide who I become involved with or not."

"You think I like this?" he asked, reaching out to grab hold of her shoulders. "Do you think I like dancing to Don's tune? I don't. It goes against everything that's in me."

"Then why?"

"My mom worked hard her whole life," he said tightly. "Thanks to my work here, my shares of Jarrod Ridge, she'll never have to work again. I bought her a condo in Orlando. She has friends. She plays golf. She gets her hair done in a fancy salon and she buys her clothes at the best boutiques in town. She takes cruises with her friends and she has *fun* for the first time in her life."

Her heart twisted in her chest as everything nebulous that she'd felt for him over the last several days solidified into something bigger. More important. Staring up into his eyes, she saw the kind of man she used to hope she'd meet. The kind who saw loyalty as a virtue. The kind who took care of his family no matter the cost to himself. The kind who put his own needs last behind everyone else in his life who mattered.

"No matter what I feel for you, or might feel for you," Christian said, "I won't take that away from her."

"I wouldn't ask you to."

"So you understand that this can't go anywhere."

"No," she said, "I don't. But I understand why you believe that."

He hissed in a breath, grabbed her hand and said, "Come with me."

She refused to move when he would have tugged her along. "Where?"

"We need to talk this out and…I want to show you something." His gaze searched hers for a long moment until he said, "Please."

Erica nodded and went with him, her fingers curled tightly around his. He led her off the concrete path and down a short slope that ran behind a short row of shops. In the distance, the forest loomed, green and filled with shadows, and he was walking right for it.

"Where are we going?" She held on to his hand and quietly enjoyed the rush of heat that linked them together.

"Thought I'd show you something here that Don Jarrod had nothing to do with building."

"You're kidding, right?" she asked as she ran to keep up with him. "I thought this was completely his."

"Most of it," he said, glancing back over his shoulder. "But this part was here first."

He led her through the trees, his steps sure as he continued on, deeper into the cool gloom. The farther they got from the resort, the quieter it became. Erica heard birds high overhead and from a distance, there was a muted roar of sound that got louder and louder as they approached.

Erica looked back over her shoulder and couldn't see the resort at all. The trees were so thick it was as if a dark green wall had been erected between them and the grounds of Jarrod Ridge.

When Christian at last came to a stop and released her hand, she was simply staggered by the beauty around her. A river rushed past them, growling and roaring over stones in its path. Lined on either side by thick stands of trees, and a narrow ribbon of rock and sand, the water was frothy and beautiful and completely untouched. It was an oasis of privacy in a sea of people and Erica loved it.

She walked closer to the water's edge, her sandals sinking and sliding on the sand. She felt the spray on her face as a soft wind kicked up, rattling the leaves of the trees until they sounded like whispered conversations.

"This was my spot when I was a kid," Christian said softly as he came up behind her. "When I needed to think, when things got bad, I came here and everything felt…all right again."

"I can see why," she said and wondered how anyone could be sad or depressed if they had somewhere so beautiful to go. She looked at him and asked, "And how many women have you brought here, I wonder?"

"Counting you?" he asked, gaze fixed on hers with

an intensity that shot a lick of flame through her center. "Just one."

"Why did you bring me?" she asked, her voice as breathless as she felt. "After everything you told me about Don and the will and everything…why did you bring me here?"

"Because," he admitted, his gaze moving over her face like a caress, "I had to."

Then he pulled her in close and kissed her.

He took her mouth with a hunger he'd never known before. Instantly, her lips parted, allowing him access, welcoming him into her warmth. He'd known, somewhere deep inside him that it would be like this with her. Known that the pulse of electricity between them would erupt into a shower of light and heat the moment he got close enough to her.

With a groan, he surrendered himself to the sensations pouring through him, refusing to think about anything beyond this moment. This kiss.

This taste of her that was filling cold, dark corners within him.

Their tongues tangled together, breath mingled and her soft sighs gave him all the encouragement he could have wanted. Sweeping one hand down her back, he traced her curves and wished he could peel her out of the dark red shirt she wore. Instead, he settled for tugging the hem of her blouse free of her crisp, white linen shorts and then slid the palm of his hand across her bare skin. She shivered as his fingers caressed the line of her spine, up and down and then up again. He needed the feel of her as badly as he needed her taste in his mouth.

Her arms came up and wrapped around his neck as she leaned into him. Her breasts flattened against his chest and he felt the hard points of her nipples pushing into him. He groaned again, felt his body go hard and ready and ground his hips against hers, looking for ease, but only managing to torture them both.

Christian kept his mouth on hers as he lifted her off her feet and deepened the kiss further. Slower, longer, hotter, he wanted all, wanted everything. For days now, his mind, his body had been clamoring for just this and now that he had his hands on her, his mouth on her, he didn't want it to end.

The roar of the river was right behind them, the insistent rush of it playing counterpoint to the thudding of his own heartbeat. When he finally tore his mouth from hers and dragged in a ragged breath, she smiled up at him.

"So much for medievalism."

His breath strangling in his lungs, he nodded. "I've never had to work so hard to stay within the rules. But I've wanted to taste you since the moment we met."

"Good to know," Erica said, moving one hand to cup his cheek in her palm. "I felt the same way. I still do. I want you, Christian."

His body tightened even further and he wouldn't have thought that possible.

"You're not making this any easier," he said, setting her back on her feet, keeping his arms around her, one hand on her bare back.

"I'm glad. It shouldn't be easy. It should be damned hard to walk away from whatever it is that's between us."

"It is. That's why I brought you here. I need to have you to myself. If only for today."

"And that would be enough for you?"

"No," he admitted, sliding both hands under her shirt now, moving over her skin to cup her breasts over the lacy cups of her bra.

She gulped an unsteady breath.

Through the lace, his thumbs and forefingers toyed with her nipples, eliciting another soft moan from her. "I've thought about tasting you, touching you. I've dreamed of having you alone and under me, over me."

"Oh, my…"

Slowly, he moved his hands until he reached the waistband of her shorts. She took a shallow breath as he deftly undid the snap and zipper.

Her gaze locked with his and Christian couldn't have looked away if it had meant his life. Suddenly the entire world, or at least all he wanted to know of it was there, in her amber-colored eyes.

"I need to touch you," he whispered, his voice almost lost in the thunder of the swift-moving river.

"Yes," she said, leaning toward him again, giving him all the welcome he needed.

He snaked one arm around her waist while his other hand dipped down, over her belly, beneath the thin elastic band of her panties. Then lower still, inch by glorious inch, past the tight curls at the juncture of her thighs. She gasped and stiffened, holding herself perfectly still as his fingers smoothed over her heat.

A low-throated groan slid from him as he felt her wet warmth and knew it was all for him. That she wanted him as desperately as he did her.

Then she jolted in his arms and a tiny, want-filled sigh slid from her lips. Her eyes closed as he dipped his hand lower still.

He touched, he caressed, he explored her delicate folds, learning her, learning what pleased her, what sent her soaring. He watched her face as he took her and her every sigh fed the flames of his own desire. He claimed her with a slick stroke across that single bud at the heart of her. That one spot that was the most sensitized and she trembled in his arms.

As sunlight played down around them and the world went about its business, Christian took Erica on a fast ride to pleasure. His fingers deft, he drove her relentlessly until she whimpered and pleaded his name on sighs torn from her throat. Her hips rocked into his hand as she sought release only he could give her. She parted her thighs wider, hoping he would take more, silently offering the invitation.

And he did. Dipping his head to the line of her throat, his lips and teeth left a trail of flames along her skin as he dipped first one finger and then another deep into her heat.

"Oh, Christian!" She swayed against him, but then held still as if afraid he'd stop.

He wouldn't. The feel of her beneath his hands was magic. Everything he'd dreamed and more. He wanted to lay her down and take her body with his completely, right here, on the soft, warm grass under the shelter of the trees. But he wouldn't. Couldn't risk someone stumbling across them. So he would settle for this stolen moment. This one instant when the two of them were alone and nothing was more important than the next sigh.

He took her higher, his fingers moving over her most tender flesh. She gasped, she sighed, she shivered against him and still he pushed her on, dragging out the sensations, taking her to the edge and then drawing her back. Lifting his head, he looked down at her and she opened her eyes as if needing to see him as tension coiled tighter and tighter within.

"Let go," he whispered, bending to brush her mouth with his. "Let go and come for me now."

Her fingers curled into the fabric of his shirt and clung to his shoulders as if she were half-afraid she would slide off the edge of the world.

"Christian..." His name came on a breath as she trembled against him.

His thumb caressed her again and then she shattered in his arms. Her body quaked and shivered, her eyes slid closed. She held on to him as pleasure rippled through her again and again until finally, the last waves died away and she was left nearly boneless.

He held her closer, wrapped both arms around her middle and held her pressed tightly to him. His own heartbeat was crashing in his chest and matched hers beat for beat. This was so much more than he had thought it would be. He felt so much more than he'd expected.

Somehow, he had thought that touching her would bring him satisfaction. That having her in his arms, sighing his name, would ease the need that had been gnawing at him for days. But it hadn't. If anything, that need was sharper now, clawing at his insides, demanding more. Demanding all.

Christian's head fell back and he stared at the sky as he realized that something incredible had just happened. Something life-changing.

But the question was, did he want his life changed— and was it too late to stop it?

For the next couple of days, Erica hardly saw Christian, but she almost didn't have time to notice. Her new life was racing straight ahead and she was forced to run just to keep up. There was a lot of work still to be done to prepare for the opening of the gala and she was working at a disadvantage, since she was coming in at the tail end. She had to catch up with Trevor's plans, and with the marketing scheme he'd devised and already had in motion.

Working with Trevor was more fun than she'd expected it to be. She knew about PR. How to market a product so that a customer would be not only slavering to have it, but instantly convinced to buy it. Working the ins and outs of a gala as big and splashy as the Jarrod Ridge affair was, at its heart, no different. There were posters to see to, artistic signs, menus for some of the out-of-town vendors and professionally shot photos, showing impossibly perfect people at play.

Jarrod Ridge was about to become the center of the food and wine industry for several weeks and Erica was right in the thick of it.

She couldn't remember being happier.

Her office on the ground floor of the Manor was bigger than her old one in San Francisco and bright with sunlight pouring in through a bank of windows. There were fresh flowers in the room, and a top-of-the-line computer and printer. She had all the assistance she needed from the employees at the business center and she had Trevor to bounce ideas off of and to argue with occasionally, as well.

What she didn't have, she thought now, was Christian.

He'd made himself scarce the last couple of days. She'd barely caught a glimpse of him. Erica stood up from behind her desk and looked out her window at the English-style garden beyond the glass. Scrubbing her hands up and down her arms, she forced herself to accept the fact that he was deliberately avoiding her. But why?

Those stolen moments beside the river rose up in her mind as they'd been doing regularly in every spare second. And in a heartbeat, she was back there again, his mouth on hers. His hand touching her intimately, pushing her into a pleasure so deep it was like nothing she'd ever known before.

It had been the most incredible encounter of her life.

So why wasn't he coming to her again?

Did he really mean to stick to Don Jarrod's ridiculous rules? Would he turn his back on her and what they might find to keep his job? Okay, yes, she could understand wanting—needing—to keep his mother safe and happy. But wasn't *he* allowed to be happy, too?

Or, she thought miserably, maybe he was happier without her. Maybe what they'd shared on the banks of the river hadn't touched him as it had her. Maybe he hadn't felt a damn thing. Maybe it hadn't meant anything from the start and he was just—

Her office door opened behind her and she whirled to face… "Christian," she said. "I was just thinking about you."

"Erica." His voice was cool, polite.

She nearly caught a chill from across the room. But two could play at this game, she told herself. If he wanted to pretend there was nothing simmering between them, then that's what they would do. Be damned if she would show him that she was hurt. That he was stomping on her heart even now with his professional air and distant tone. No, she wouldn't give him the satisfaction.

"Can I help you?" Her words were as polite as his. Her tone every bit as cold.

"I've come to introduce you to—"

"Me," another man said as he walked into the office and looked at her. "I'm Blake Jarrod."

"It's nice to meet you," she said, maintaining the professional manner she'd begun with. Erica saw no warm welcome in his eyes, so she wasn't going to act as though they were any two siblings greeting each other.

Blake studied her and could see what his twin had already mentioned to him. Their newest sister did have the look of the Jarrods about her, so there was clearly no mistake made. He could see it in the defiant tilt of her chin. In the flash of her eyes. Hell, she probably had more of Don in her than Blake did.

But that didn't mean that he'd welcome her into the family like the prodigal daughter. Or that she deserved a share of the estate. Being blood didn't mean jack if you didn't earn your place, he told himself. Everyone else might be willing to give her a chance, but he wasn't so easily taken in. She'd have to prove herself to him.

Not that he had anything against her personally. And judging from what Melissa had had to say on the subject, he would probably like her. Eventually. But for right now, she was the intruder. Pushing her way into a family already hip-deep in problems and not really needing any extras.

"Getting along all right, I see," he said, giving her office a quick scan.

"Everyone's been very helpful," Erica told him, then came around her desk and took a few steps closer. "Look, I know how hard this is for all of us. And I'm not expecting us to be one big happy family anytime soon."

He folded his arms across his chest and nodded.

"I do, however, expect you to give me a fair chance," she said.

"You do."

Erica looked directly at him and refused to be cowed by his steely stare. She'd already been warned that Blake would be the hardest nut to crack, so to speak. That this one of her new brothers would be the least welcoming. So she would stand her ground and if she needed to show him that she meant to make this place her home, then that's what she'd do.

Besides, Christian was standing right there, watching her, and she wasn't about to look weak or pitiful in front of him.

"That's right. Just as you would any new employee," Erica said. "I think that's fair."

Blake thought about it for a long moment before he nodded and walked forward, offering his hand. "It is fair. Okay, a chance it is."

"Thanks." Erica shook his hand and stepped back.

"Now, I've got to go find Gavin and talk to him about some business. If you two will excuse me…"

Blake left, shutting the door behind him and suddenly Erica and Christian were alone. Silence dragged out for what seemed like forever. Finally though, Christian said, "You handled him well."

"Thanks," she said, her words clipped, "is that all?"

"Erica…"

"I really don't have time to talk right now, Christian.

Trevor's expecting to see the new poster I've designed for the gala and—"

"I've missed you."

She whipped her head around to glare at him. "Couldn't have been easy to miss seeing me. I've been right here."

He blew out a breath and took the few steps separating them. Now that he was closer, Erica could see the shadows under his eyes and realized he hadn't been sleeping well. That made two of them. She wanted to reach out and touch him, but wasn't sure he would accept it, so she kept her wants buried under a layer of anger.

"It's complicated," he said.

"Not as far as I can see. You haven't spoken to me since…"

"You think I don't want to?" His voice was low and hard. "You really believe I'm not thinking about you every damn minute?"

Her heartbeat felt faint and fast. The look on his face was haunted, his eyes were blazing with fury and desire. "How would I know that when you've been avoiding me?"

"Because if I don't avoid you, this is what's going to happen." He closed the distance between them, grabbed her and pulled her close, wrapping his arms around her so tightly she could hardly draw breath.

And she didn't care.

Didn't care because his mouth was on hers, his breath driving into her mouth, his hands scooping up her back into her hair. His body pressed into hers. She felt the hard, thick ridge of him that proved exactly what he was feeling for her.

She moved in even closer, giving herself up to the feelings only he could engender. Her body was hot, her blood felt as if it were boiling in her veins. So when he released her abruptly, Erica staggered back a step before she recovered her balance.

Lifting one hand to her lips, she stared at him, trying to understand just what kind of game he was playing. And why she was allowing it.

"Yes," he said, his eyes fierce, his voice a deep groan of need, "I want you. So damn much just being around you is painful." He shoved one hand across the top of his head. "But you've got enough going on in your life right now. You don't need this as an added distraction."

Erica blinked at him. She couldn't believe what he was saying and wasn't sure he believed it, either. "So you're backing off for my sake, is that it? Making a grand sacrifice so poor Erica doesn't get confused by too many things at once?"

He winced, either at her words or the sharp slap of how they were delivered. "All I'm saying—"

She interrupted him because she'd heard enough. "I'm sick and tired of people deciding what's best for me. My father and brothers did it for years. And if you think I'm going to allow *you* to jump in and do the same, then you couldn't be more wrong."

She was trembling, her body shaking and quivering, not only from the rush of anger. Once again, he'd turned her body into an inferno of desire only to shut it down before it could fully erupt.

"That's not what I'm trying to do," he ground out.

Frustration and fury mingled inside her.

"Oh, no. All you're saying is thanks but no thanks. You've made that clear." She turned her back on him and walked back to her desk. Once she was safely behind the rosewood barrier, she looked at him again. "Well, I'm just so grateful for your help, Christian. With so many things going on in my life, I don't know what I would have done without you there to help me keep things straight."

He looked just as angry as she felt, and she was glad to see it. At least she knew that his ridiculous decision to pull away from her was making him as crazy as it was her.

"Erica, damn it—"

"Just stop it, okay? I've got a lot of work to do and I'm guessing you do, too."

He stared at her for a long second then nodded as if accepting that the conversation was over. "Fine. We'll leave it. For now. But neither one of us is going anywhere, so you can be damn sure this isn't finished."

"Isn't it?" Erica asked. "How is it that *you* suddenly get to decide how this relationship will go? When did you get the controlling vote?"

"Excuse me?"

He sounded angry—his voice was low and taut. *Well, good*, she thought. Why should she be the only one furious here?

"Do you seriously think so little of me to believe that I'm incapable of making my own decisions?"

"Of course not. That isn't what I meant at all."

"It's what you said. Poor Erica. Too many new things in her life."

"Damn it, you're deliberately misunderstanding."

"Oh, I understand more than you think I do."

"What's that supposed to mean?"

"Just that this isn't about *me* at all, Christian. You can tell yourself that if it makes you feel better. But this is really about you playing by a dead man's rules."

A muscle ticked in his jaw and she saw the flare of anger in his eyes. She recognized it because she knew that same emotion was shining in her own. She'd spent the past several days torn between anger and misery, but now the fury was spilling over.

He reached for her, but she scuttled back, not trusting herself to allow him to touch her right now. She might shatter. Need swam inside her and battled her own pride. It was a toss-up at the moment which would win.

"I told you," he said, letting his hands fall to his sides, "I can't risk what I spent my life building. But it's also true that you've got too much going on in your own life right now. You don't need me making things even more complicated."

"Oh, stop it," she whispered, shaking her head. She'd already trusted him too much, risked too much. She couldn't chance feeling even more. Trusting more. He'd already pushed her aside. How much clearer could he make himself?

"Wish I could," he admitted, coming around her desk, walking closer and closer still. "Wish to hell I could put you and what's between us out of my mind, but it won't go."

She laughed sadly, thinking of the past few days when he'd avoided her at all costs. "It seems you've been doing a fine job of that."

"No. You're in my mind all the damn time. You haunt me, Erica, and I'm not sure how to deal with that." He reached out, and this time she didn't move away. Couldn't make herself do it.

He cupped her face between his palms. Staring into her eyes, he said, "What's between us won't be denied and neither one of us can wish it away."

"Can't we?" she asked, her voice soft as she met his gaze searchingly. "Isn't that what's been happening lately?"

"No," he countered. "This is what's been happening."

Then he kissed her. Hard and deep, pouring into that kiss everything she'd been needing for so long. Her head swam, her heartbeat quickened into a racing gallop and by the time he broke away, she was laboring for breath.

Yet at the same time a tiny corner of her heart was erecting barriers, ready to defend her.

"Don't," he said softly. "I can feel you pulling away even when I'm holding you."

"Haven't you been doing the same thing these last few days?"

"No," he answered, releasing her and taking a step back. "I'm doing what I have to do."

"Because you won't risk caring for me."

"Because this is my life," he reminded her, and his features were hard.

"It's my life, too," she told him, stiffening her spine. "And I won't be used then discarded on a whim. You can't run hot and then cold on me, Christian. I refuse to play that game."

"You're wrong about me," he said tightly. "I'm not playing games, Erica. I wouldn't do that to either one of us."

She scraped her hands up and down her arms, trying to chase away the chill that was swamping her. But it was bone-deep and she was suddenly sure that she'd never be really warm again. What she felt for Christian was going nowhere. Because he would continue to refuse what lay between them. Once again, Erica thought sadly, she just wasn't wanted badly enough.

When he was gone, Erica slumped into her desk chair, turned it around and stared out at a sunlit day that had gone, for her at least, suddenly dark.

Eight

Despite their argument, over the next week, Christian spent time with Erica every day. He continued to be her guide as she grew more and more accustomed to her new life. But somehow he managed to keep their conversations centered on business, or the resort itself. He refused to bring up anything personal and she must have come to the same conclusion. She was polite. Cool. She treated him as she would have a distant acquaintance.

And every minute he was with her was a session in torture.

He'd never wanted anyone with the fierce desperation he did her. Thoughts of her plagued him constantly. He couldn't lose himself in his work anymore. Couldn't stroll through the Manor without seeing her, hearing her—or hearing someone else talk about her.

She'd charmed the staff and had settled into her new position as if she'd been born to it. And in a way, he supposed, she had. She was a Jarrod, after all. Which was the major problem for him.

If she weren't a member of the Jarrod family, he wouldn't be doing his best to ignore her.

Stopping by her office, he knocked, then walked inside to find her hunched over her keyboard, gaze fixed on the screen. Even here, he thought, when she was unaware that anyone was watching her, she looked... alluring. Her hair was tucked behind her ears and long, twisted shards of gold hung from her lobes. She was chewing at her bottom lip as her fingers flew over the keys and didn't look away even when she reached out blindly for a cup of coffee on her desk.

She'd given herself up to this job. This place. She'd jumped in with both feet and, true to her word, was definitely making a place for herself.

He wished that place was with him. But damned if he could see a way to make that happen.

As if she sensed his presence, Erica looked up then. Backlit from the window behind her, her amber eyes were shadowed, but he could still see the trepidation on her features as she looked at him. "Hi. Was there something you needed?"

"Loaded question," he muttered, then said more loudly, "Actually, yeah. There is. I wanted to know if you approved the design for the gala's setup on the main lawn."

"Yes, I did. I sent the papers over to Trevor this morning."

"Fine. I'll check with him again. He couldn't find them earlier, but that's not saying anything. He probably misfiled them."

She smiled slightly. "That does sound like Trevor."

"You like him," Christian said.

"It's impossible not to," Erica told him as her smile slowly slipped away. "He's got this flair for living that I really admire. He is who he is and makes no excuses for it. He simply lives and enjoys every minute of it."

Christian stiffened a little at the inherent comparison between himself and the easygoing Trevor Jarrod. "Trying to tell me something?"

She glanced up at him and shook her head, her soft hair swinging in a gentle arc that made Christian want to reach out and bury his fingers in the softness. "No, Christian, I'm not. I think we've already said everything there was to say."

"Impossible," he told her, walking toward her desk. "We couldn't have, because there's still too much unsaid between us."

"And it should probably stay that way," she said.

"Maybe," he agreed, reminding himself that it was *he* who'd put up the wall between them. He had been the one to take the first step back from what they might have found. And though it infuriated him to acknowledge even privately that she might have had a point when she accused him of being unwilling to face up to a dead man's wishes…she hadn't been far wrong.

If Don Jarrod were still alive, it would be different. He could go to the man, tell him how he felt about Erica. Make the old bastard see that she was right in saying that the fraternization clause was medieval. But with Don gone, the board of directors was in charge, and with the codicil in Don's will insisting that the clause remain in effect, they wouldn't be making changes anytime soon.

And how the hell could he go to the Jarrod siblings and insist that *they* change it? He couldn't be sure that they wouldn't side with their father.

Christian felt as if his hands were tied and his heart was being ripped in two. What he wanted was vying desperately with what he'd spent his life working for.

"Let's not do this again, Christian," she said quietly as she stood and came around her desk. "At the very least, we can stop torturing each other."

He tucked his hands into his slacks pockets to keep from grabbing her. God, he missed the feel of her pressed against him. The taste of her. The scent of her. He was making himself crazy with wanting her.

Then she reached up and smoothed his hair back from his forehead and the soft slide of her fingertips against his skin sent flames rushing through him. He inhaled sharply, deeply, and she instantly let her hand drop to her side again.

"Sorry," she said with a shrug she no doubt meant to look nonchalant. "As angry as I am at you, it seems I still have to remind myself not to touch you."

"I know the feeling all too well," he admitted, calling on every ounce of his will to keep from holding her and damn the rest of the world. Screw his job. Screw the Jarrod family. Screw Don Jarrod in particular for creating this hell for the two of them.

"I guess we'll just have to work on it, won't we?"

"Right." He nodded, but it cost him. "I'll just go check with Trevor about those papers."

"I'll go with you," she said. Tugging her white, long-sleeved shirt down at the hem, she smoothed her denim skirt.

Her legs looked long and tanned and her feet were tucked into dark blue heels that made her legs look even longer. Hell, she didn't even have to try to make him crazy.

Erica walked past him into the hall and he fell into step beside her. Blake and Gavin were standing near the elevator, locked in a conversation that was suddenly halted when they drew near.

"Hey, guys," Christian said. "What's going on?"

Blake shot Erica a wary look and said, "Nothing. Just talking. What're you two up to?"

Erica said, "Just checking on some paperwork with Trevor."

"Right. Well." The elevator door opened and Blake stepped in. "We'll see you later."

As the doors whisked closed again, they both heard Gavin say, "For God's sake, Blake, lighten up with Erica, will you? She's not the enemy."

"That went well," Erica said wryly as they continued on to Trevor's office.

"Blake will come around." Christian took her

arm and pulled her to a stop. "It's a big change for everyone."

She looked down at his hand on her arm until he released her. Then she shifted her gaze to his. "I don't mind Blake's feelings. At least he's honest."

Heading into Trevor's office alone, Erica didn't look back at him. So she didn't see Christian's dark scowl as he was left standing alone.

The main spa room at the Ridge was so opulent it was nearly decadent. Which made it perfect. A curve of aquamarine water followed the circumference of the room. Jets built into the walls of the pool produced frothy bubbles of pure relaxation and the only sounds were from the jets and the rhythmic splash of the overhead waterfalls spraying heated water down into the waiting pool.

Erica felt loose and limber and almost guilty for taking an entire day to do nothing but be pampered. Still, since it had been Melissa's idea to have a quiet day of sisterly bonding, Erica thought she could let the guilt go just this once. Besides, after the long week she'd had, it felt good to just relax, away from the Manor, away from Christian.

"You're seriously making us all look bad," Melissa told her with a sigh. "I mean, really, you don't have to be Jarrod Family Member of the Year right off the bat."

Erica smiled and hid the hurt that seemed to be a constant companion. Yes, she was making great strides at her new job. Her brothers and sister were coming around—she'd even managed to talk to Blake without him glaring at her. And she'd had dozens of compliments on her plans for the splashy welcome she'd designed for the opening of the gala.

For the first time in her life, Erica felt as though she was being accepted for who and what she was. For what she could contribute. And it felt great.

Or would have, if there wasn't a shadow clinging to her thoughts. Christian hardly spoke to her anymore. Not since that last kiss they'd shared in her office a week ago. She saw him at the Manor, of course. The offices were all too close together for them to completely avoid each other.

Though that might have been easier all the way around. How much harder was it to see him and not be able to touch him? Talk to him? But she refused to be the kind of woman who threw herself at a man when he had already made it clear that there couldn't be anything between them.

"Okay, what's wrong?"

"Hmm? What?" Erica jolted as she realized her thoughts had wandered off while Melissa was talking to her. "Nothing. I'm just thinking about work."

"Uh-huh." Melissa shook her head and reached out to pat Erica's shoulder.

The two of them had indulged in a luxury spa treatment. They'd already been through the facials, the massages and now, they were stretched out side by side in the narrow curve of the pool, relaxing. Or they were supposed to be.

"I know that look," Melissa said. "And it's not a 'work' look. It's a 'man' look. So spill."

She automatically shook her head. She'd never been one to share secrets with her girlfriends and there was simply no way she wanted her new sister to know that she was lusting after a man who wasn't interested. "I really don't think—"

Melissa gave her a dramatic pout. "What's the point of having a sister if you can't bare your soul and get free advice—or sarcasm, as the situation demands."

In spite of everything, Erica smiled. It did feel good to have a sister. Even two weeks ago, she never would have believed that she'd be able to use the words "my sister" in a sentence. Yet here they were, and astonishingly enough, the two of them had actually formed a bond that Erica hoped would only get stronger with time.

Sister wasn't just a word anymore. It was real. And it was good.

"Okay," she said, and glanced around to make sure they were still alone.

"Relax. The place is ours for the afternoon. I run the spa, remember?"

"Right." Erica lifted one arm and slid it through the water, letting the jetted bubbles pulse against her skin. "Okay, say there was a man I'm having a problem with."

"Yes, let's say that." Melissa leaned back and floated, allowing more of the jets to beat against her body. "Now let's say some more."

"Okay, this man, he's interested, but he's not willing to get involved."

"What's his problem?"

"It's a long story," Erica said, not wanting to give Christian's name or his reasons for pulling back from her. She wasn't sure if they knew about the fraternization clause.

"One you don't want to share."

"Not exactly."

"Is he married?"

"No! of course not!" Erica frowned at the other woman. "If he was, I wouldn't be making myself nuts over him."

"Okay, so do you want this man?"

"Yes, damn it."

Melissa laughed. "So go get him. Or at least try."

"What about dignity?" Erica countered. "Pride? Am I supposed to chase him down like a dog with him protesting the whole time?"

Straightening up, Melissa shook her wet hair back from her face and gave Erica a pitying look. "Little sister, men are simple creatures. He wants you. That's the point here. He's trying to stay away for whatever reason, but he doesn't want to. So make it a little more difficult for him to ignore you. For heaven's sake, why would you make it easier on him?"

"I don't know…" Erica sighed and shifted in the water, letting the heated water push into her back, easing tension she hadn't even really been aware of.

"Up to you of course," Melissa told her. "But for me, if there was a guy I wanted, I'd go get him."

Her words were said so forcefully Erica had to wonder if there was a particular man her sister was talking about. But an instant later, the timer for the jets shut off and silence dropped over them.

"I'll think about it," Erica said, climbing out of the water and reaching for a fluffy white towel.

"Less thinking, more kissing is probably the way you want to go," Melissa advised, "but maybe that's just me."

Maybe Melissa was right, Erica thought as she and her sister toweled off and moved toward the locker room to get dressed. Because really, why was she making it easier for Christian to ignore her? Could be that what she *should* be doing was spending more time with him, not less. Talk to him. Lean into him. Keep him so close that he wouldn't be able to pull away from her.

After all, ignoring him hadn't hurt him and had been driving her insane. So, she'd turn the tables on him. Take Melissa's advice and make him so miserable that he wouldn't be able to avoid her. And, since she'd just spent the last three hours being buffed and polished and styled, today was the perfect day to set this new and much more interesting plan in motion.

Christian threw a rock into the river and watched it hit the water and sink. Just how he felt, he thought. He'd been carrying around a sinking feeling inside him for the last two weeks and it was only getting worse.

Being here at Jarrod Ridge had always given him a sense of satisfaction that he'd found nowhere else. He'd studied back east and had been eager to get back to Colorado. He'd traveled the world and never found another spot as beautiful as this one. But now...

There was an unsettled feeling inside him.

And its name was Erica Prentice.

Hell, he couldn't even enjoy standing alongside the river anymore. Because he saw her here, now. She was everydamnwhere in Aspen, and no matter how hard he tried, he couldn't get away from her.

"Well," a too familiar voice said from behind him, "you look furious."

He turned around to watch Erica approach him. The sunlight was fading as twilight edged closer. She wore a short, lemon-yellow skirt that stopped midthigh and a pale green short-sleeved T-shirt that displayed her tanned, toned arms and clung to her narrow waist. Her hair was soft and shining in the last of the light and her eyes were locked on his.

"So," she asked as she came nearer, "did you want to be alone with your fury or can you stand some company?"

"Alone," he ground out, because he knew if she came any closer, he wouldn't be able to stop himself from reaching for her.

"That's a shame, because I prefer company," she said. She whipped her hair back from her face and continued down the slope, passing within inches of him as she walked to the water's edge.

"What're you doing here, Erica?"

She glanced back at him and shrugged. "I came to look at the river."

"And you could only see the river from here. This one spot. On the whole resort."

She smiled slowly. "I like this spot."

His hands fisted at his sides and he deliberately relaxed them, taking a long, deep breath into his lungs at the same time. Unfortunately, that only brought him a whiff of her scent, which made his insides tighten into knots. She smelled like peaches and flowers and all things soft and beautiful.

"Fine," he said. "Enjoy the view. I'll go."

"Okay, so will I." She turned and headed back toward him.

"What are you playing at?" he demanded when she stood right in front of him.

She shook her head and looked up into his eyes. "I'm done playing, Christian. No more games. No more teasing. I'm here because I want you and you want me."

His teeth ground together and he hissed in a breath, hoping to find some equilibrium. He didn't.

She lifted both hands to his shirt front and smoothed her palms over his chest.

His body went from hard to aching in under a second. He caught her hands in his and stilled them. Then he stared into her eyes and whispered, "Why are you doing this?"

"Because you won't," she said and went up on her toes to slant her mouth over his. Once, twice, a soft brush of her lips to his and Christian felt the heat of her rush through him.

He knew he was a dead man. He had to have her.

Couldn't have turned away now if someone had a gun to his head. She was everything he wanted, needed. She was all he could think about. All he cared about. It didn't matter if he would regret this later or not. Or, if being with her would only make the situation between them harder.

For now, he was lost.

He grabbed her then, as if half-afraid she might disappear on him if he didn't hold on to her tightly. Pulling her up close to him, he took her mouth with a desperation he'd felt clawing at him for days. Again and again, his tongue delved deep, claiming her in a mimicry of what his body wanted to be doing to hers. In and out, he dazzled, he took, he gave, his heartbeat racing, his blood pumping, he gave himself over to the demands of his body, clamoring to meet her demands.

As a soft summer wind caressed them both, Christian took the hem of her shirt and pulled it up and over her head. She threw her head back and laughed in delight as the air touched her heated skin. In that moment, Erica looked more beautiful to him than she ever had before. He unhooked her bra and spilled her breasts out into the palms of his hands.

She sucked in a breath as he cupped her, rolling her nipples between his thumbs and forefingers. She sighed, arching into him, offering herself to him as the sun's last golden rays played across her skin.

Her eager response fed the fires within him and Christian groaned, bent his head and took first one nipple and then the other into his mouth. Her skin was soft and smooth and smelled of peaches. His lips and tongue and teeth nibbled and suckled at her, drawing sighs and moans from deep in her throat. Her fingers slid through his hair, holding his head to her, as if worried that he would stop, that he would suddenly pull away and tell her no, they weren't going to do this.

But that wasn't even a glimmer in his brain.

They'd passed that line and there was no going back.

If he didn't have her *now,* he knew he'd die of the want.

With one last, lingering draw on her nipple, Christian straightened, caught her hand in his and said, "Come over here."

"What? What?" Dazed and unsteady, Erica followed him, her hand tucked into his. "Where?"

"Right here," he said, picking a blanket up off the ground and spreading it out beneath the trees.

She laughed a little, surprised. "You came prepared?"

He grinned, feeling lighter than he had in weeks. "Sometimes I sleep out here on warm nights. Good to have a blanket handy."

"It is," she agreed and went to him eagerly. She wrapped her arms around his neck and held on, kissing him deeply, slowly. Until finally, Christian growled, pulled his head back and lay her down on the blanket.

"Let's get you out of those clothes."

"You, too," she urged and immediately wiggled out

of her skirt and pushed her panties down and off. She kicked out of her sandals and lay across the pale blue quilt like an offering from the gods.

Christian took seconds to strip and join her on the blanket, going up on one elbow to kiss her while his left hand stroked up and down the line of her body. He defined her curves, explored every valley and took the time to tease her rigid nipples until she moaned into his mouth.

Her hand moved over his back, sliding across his shoulders and down the length of his spine. Every touch inflamed him until his body was so hard and tight, he could hardly think beyond the need hammering at his mind, his heart.

He slid his hand down over her belly and past the nest of curls to find her center. She gasped and lifted her hips for his touch. He obliged, sliding his fingertips across those heated folds, finding her damp warmth and realizing that she was as ready for him as he was for her. He dipped one finger inside her and stroked those inner muscles until she whispered his name with a hunger that matched his own.

"Christian, don't wait. Take me now, be inside me now. I need this. I need *you*."

"No more waiting," he promised and shifted to cover her body with his. He knelt between her thighs and parted them wider, opening her up to his gaze.

She twisted beneath him. "Christian," she said, licking her lips, "please. Now."

"Now." He pushed his body into hers with one long

stroke and instantly experienced the wild rush of being a part of the only woman who mattered to him.

She was tight and hot and caressed his length every time he withdrew only to surge forward again. Her legs came up, wrapped around his middle and took him deeper on every stroke. She curled her fists into the blanket beneath her and lifted her hips, rocking into him, following the rhythm he set and matching him move for move.

"Open your eyes," he ordered, staring down into her face as he took her. Her eyes flew open and met his. He read his own desire reflected back at him and saw in those amber depths the passion he'd waited too long to see.

She released the blanket so she could touch him, scraped her palms up and down his chest, up and over his back and dug her fingernails into his shoulders as he increased their pace. Hips pistoning, he took her higher, faster than either of them had ever been before.

Together, they raced toward a completion that had been waiting for them for weeks and together, they crashed over the edge and fell.

Nine

Erica was spent.

Every cell in her body was whimpering with release and pure pleasure. Her legs were trembling and her arms felt as if they weighed a ton. Christian was sprawled on top of her and though he was heavy, she didn't want him to move. Didn't want to lose this connection they had. She wanted to keep his body joined to hers for as long as possible.

Staring up through the thick branches overhead, she spotted small slices of a deep purple sky. The sun was down and the first stars were coming out. Beside them, the river rushed on, and here, on this blanket, the world was standing still.

"I want to roll off of you," he muttered, his voice

muffled against her skin. "But I don't think I can move."

She smiled, delighted that she'd brought such a man to his knees, so to speak. Christian was more than she'd thought when she first met him. Then he'd seemed so locked away, so suit and tie and cool distance. Now she knew what he kept hidden beneath that very businesslike exterior. And she didn't ever want to lose him.

"I don't want you to move anyway. I love the feel of you against me. In me."

Love.

Erica's breath caught in her chest and she smiled to herself as she realized it was true. She did love him. Why hadn't she realized it before? It all seemed so simple now. So clear. It didn't matter how fast it had all happened. It was as if she'd been heading here. To Colorado, to *him,* her whole life. Days, weeks, time had nothing to do with it. When it was right, it was right, she told herself firmly and gently stroked her hands up and down his broad, muscular back.

He groaned and lifted himself up onto his elbows. Looking down into her eyes, he rolled his hips against hers and she sucked in a gulp of air. His body stirred inside her, thickening, hardening. She sighed at the sensation and suddenly she was more than ready for him.

"You touch me and I can't think," he admitted, moving again, slowly, pushing deeply into her.

But in a heartbeat he went perfectly still and stared

down into her eyes. "Can't think. *Didn't* think. Erica, we didn't use any protection."

She gasped, stunned that the thought had never even occurred to her. She'd never done anything so irresponsible in her life.

"I'm sorry. I should have— Damn it."

"Stop," she said quickly, reaching up to cup his face with her palm. "It was my mistake as well as yours. But as long as we're both healthy, it should be all right."

"I am, I swear," he said, concern etched on his face. "But are you sure you won't get—"

"Pregnant?" she finished for him. "I can't be absolutely positive, of course, but it's the wrong time of the month, so…"

"Good. That's good."

But he didn't sound relieved, she thought. He sounded almost…sorry.

"But we shouldn't risk it again."

"Probably not," she admitted, "but if you pull out of me now, I'll have to kill you."

He grinned, lowered his head and kissed her. "I'll risk it if you will."

"Oh, yes," she said, sliding her hands up and down his back, over his shoulders and down the front of his chest. "Thinking's overrated anyway."

"Right," he murmured, dipping his head for a kiss. "Just feel. Just experience."

"Experience is good," she agreed, already feeling the fires burning, building within.

"New experience is even better," he said and leaned back, wrapping his arms around her, drawing her up with him, keeping their bodies joined. He sat back on his heels, with Erica on his lap.

She gasped and threw her head back, loving the feel of him impaling her so deeply. Instinctively, she twisted her hips, grinding her body against his, increasing the friction between them until he groaned her name and clamped both hands at her hips, holding her still.

In the soft light of the early evening, Erica looked down at him. Cupping his face in her palms, she took a kiss and then one more before sliding her hands down his neck to his shoulders. Then she moved on him, easing herself up and down in a slow, lazy rhythm, driving them both relentlessly onward. His hands at her hips, he kept his gaze locked with hers as she moved, taking him deep, releasing him, only to reclaim him again.

Over and over, as tension built, as need spiraled inside her, she moved, rocking, swaying, twisting her hips at their joining. Her hands at his shoulders, she felt it when he neared completion and surrendered to her own climax. As the first, electric ripples of pleasure dazzled through her, she heard him shout her name just before he let go and gave himself completely to her.

It was perfect.

What could have been hours passed before Christian said, "Are you cold?"

A chill swept along her spine, but it had nothing to do with the cold. It was his deep whisper resonating in her ear that affected her so. "No. Not cold."

"Still…" Christian reached across her, grabbed the edge of the blanket and drew it up over her.

Erica snuggled into his side and laid her head on his chest. Running one hand across his warm skin, she tangled her fingers through the soft dark hair until he laughed and the rumble sounded loud in his chest. "Touch me like that and we're not going to ever go back to the Manor. I'll have to keep you here all night."

"Not a very good threat," she admitted with a smile. "It actually sounds fabulous." She tipped her face up to look into his eyes. "I don't think I could ever have enough of you."

He lifted his head, gave her a quick, hard kiss, then lay back down again, one arm tightening around her, holding her close. "I don't know what to say to you."

"Say you don't regret it."

"I'd be a damn fool if I did," he muttered.

She smiled to herself and sighed a little, enjoying the moment. The soft wind rustling through the trees, the grumbling river just a few feet away and the soft summer night close around them. It was all perfect. Her life finally felt…right.

"Not that I'm complaining," he said, "but how did you know to find me here?"

"Hmm? Oh, Melissa suggested it. She said you came out here a lot on clear nights."

His hand on her arm stilled and Erica sensed that something had changed, though he hadn't said a word. Silent tension spilled out between them and though he was still beside her, Erica knew that he was already pulling away. "Christian?"

He scrubbed one hand across his face, released her and sat up to stare out at the river. "Melissa? Melissa knows you were going to come to me?"

"She knows I was looking for you, sure." Now she was cold. Despite the warmth of the evening air she felt as though ice crystals were settling on her skin. She tugged the edge of the blanket around her and stretched out one hand to touch his back.

He flinched at the contact.

"Great. That's just great." He stood up, grabbed his jeans and tugged them on. Then he snatched up her clothes from where they'd fallen and tossed them to her. "Get dressed."

Hurt and feeling at a complete loss, she only stared at him. "What is wrong with you? Why are you acting like this?"

"Unbelievable." He muttered something else under his breath, but she couldn't catch it.

Erica grabbed the clothing he'd tossed her. She slipped her bra on, then tugged her T-shirt on over her head. When she stood up to pull on her panties and skirt, she turned her head to look at him. He was searching for his shirt and finally found it hanging from a tree limb where he must have thrown it earlier.

Disgusted, he snatched it down and Erica was more confused than ever, so she blurted, "What is going on?"

He pulled his shirt on then ran his fingers through his hair. Glaring at her he said, "I told you, I couldn't be with you. I work for the Jarrod resort. *You're* a Jarrod.

Word of this gets out, I'll lose everything. And what do you do? You tell your sister."

Erica inhaled sharply, feeling as though he'd slapped her. This was what had him so tense? Knowing that she'd spoken to Melissa? Was he really that worried that someone might know they were together? Was his job really that important?

Stung to her soul, she snapped, "Your reputation's safe, Christian. Melissa didn't know why I wanted to see you. It's not like I advertised or printed a pamphlet alerting the residents of Jarrod Ridge that I was going to try to seduce a man who's been trying to keep me at arm's length!"

"Damn it, Erica…"

"Relax," she told him hotly. "You don't want people to know you were with me? Rest easy then, because I'm in no hurry for anyone to find out about this moment."

He faced her and though his teeth were gritted, he still managed to say, "It's not that I don't want them to know. I can't *let* them know."

"Oh." She nodded and gave him a wry smile. "Big difference. Thanks for clearing that up."

"You don't get it, do you?" He stood, legs far apart, arms folded across his chest as if he were trying to hold himself in place. "I've worked my whole damn life for what I've got here. I won't risk it. Won't lose it. You can't understand because you've always had this…" He threw his arms wide as if taking in all of Jarrod Ridge. "With either the Prentice family or the

Jarrods, you're one of them. I don't have that. I *made* my way on my own."

"And I haven't?" She snorted in disgust. "You saw my office in San Francisco. Bottom of the food chain. You know why? Because my father never wanted me involved in the Prentice family business. So what I had I made. On my own. And coming here didn't change that."

"Erica—"

"No, you had your say. Now it's my turn. I told you what it was like where I grew up. Never accepted. Never let into the inner circle. It's only here that I've begun to find my way and even then, I wasn't exactly met by a ticker tape parade."

He shook his head and sighed. "That's different. Whether the Jarrods were happy about it or not, you were one of them. You belonged. Like I said, you don't get it."

"I'm not one of them. I might be. One day. I hope so. But if that happens it'll be because I *made* it happen," she countered. "I wasn't handed anything. You think it was easy to come here? It wasn't. I walked out on the only family I knew. I gave up my job, my home, my *life* to try for something new. Something better."

"I'm not going to argue with you," he told her quietly.

"Of course not," Erica muttered. "You might lose."

"I'm doing what I have to do and you'll never understand it."

"Oh, I get it," she said softly. "Finally I get it. You're a coward."

He took the two steps separating them and grabbed hold of her upper arms. His hands were strong, each of his fingers digging into her skin as he dragged her up on her toes, so they could be eye to eye. "I'm no coward and you don't know what you're talking about."

"Yes, I do," she said. Erica wasn't afraid of him. Even with his eyes nearly glowing with fury, he wouldn't hurt her. It wasn't in him. He was a closed-up man hiding a passionate nature, but that passion didn't include brute force. "I can see it in your eyes. You're already pulling away from me, from what we found, planning on how you can avoid me in the future."

He let her go instantly and backed up, muttering under his breath. Then he said, "When we're around others, nothing has to change. We just won't be doing… this again."

"Oh, is that all?"

God, how was she breathing? Everything inside her was still and cold. Her lungs, her heart. Even the blood running through her veins felt icy.

Erica grabbed her sandals and hopped on one foot then the other to tug them on. Once she was dressed completely, she threw her hair back from her face and stared daggers at him. "After what we just experienced you can actually stand there and say to me that you don't want us to be together? That you'll walk away from this? From what we might have?"

* * *

No, Christian thought wildly, he didn't want to say that. Didn't want to think it. With Erica, he'd found more peace, more excitement than he'd thought possible. When he held her, she was the world. He couldn't imagine never having her with him again. Couldn't even see his life without her in it.

These last few hours had been more precious than anything he'd ever known before. From the moment she'd approached him, it was as if they'd stepped into some dream world where they were the only two beings in existence. He'd forgotten his hard and fast rules. He'd turned his back on what he'd made of himself over the years and lost the essence of who and what he was in her. The magic of her.

But magic wasn't real.

And eventually, dreamers woke up.

He wanted her desperately. But if he acted on what he wanted, then he stood to lose everything he'd ever worked for. Everything that had made him what he was. How could he turn his back on his life? On the man he'd become? If he did, what would he have left?

Who would he be?

"You're going to do it, aren't you?" she whispered. "Even after everything that happened tonight, you're going to be the good corporate drone and go back to your cubicle."

He sighed. What the hell could he say to her? He couldn't even explain it to himself. "Erica…"

"No, don't bother." Her voice was low, almost lost in the roar of the river. But somehow he heard every word and felt the power of them hit home as if each one was a blade.

"You're going to regret tossing me aside," she said.

He stared into her eyes and couldn't quite bring himself to tell her that he already *did* regret it. Standing here, so close and yet so far away from her, he felt as if all the life was draining out of his body. But he couldn't say what she wanted—needed—to hear.

"You'll regret it, but it'll be too late. I feel sorry for you, Christian. Because I would have loved you forever." With a sad shake of her head, she turned and walked away from him.

Christian watched her go and felt his heart go with her.

She was gone the next morning. Back to San Francisco on the family jet. According to Melissa, Erica was only going back for a visit, but Christian couldn't help but wonder if he'd managed to drive her away from her legacy.

Two days later, he felt on edge. He was miserable. He hadn't slept. Couldn't close his eyes without seeing her. Work wasn't the salve it had always been. He couldn't concentrate on any single task because his mind kept drifting to Erica and the way she'd looked at him just before she walked away.

He never should have let her go.

"What the hell is wrong with you?"

Christian shook his head and glared at Trevor. They were in Trevor's office and had been working on the layout for the gala and somewhere in there, Christian's mind had taken a sharp left turn. "Nothing. Can we just finish this? I've got other things to take care of."

"You know what? Never mind. I'll finish it myself."

"Good." For the first time in years, Christian wasn't interested in Jarrod Ridge or its gala. He didn't care about the tourists flocking to Aspen or the businesses depending on the Ridge to increase their profits. He was damn sick and tired of living his life by the wants and needs of the Jarrod family.

Hell, he was still following Don Jarrod's edicts even after the man was in his grave. So Christian's life had now come to the point where a dead man was controlling his actions.

Was he really going to allow this to continue? Could he really risk losing the only woman who'd ever gotten under his guard?

Would he give up his future to assuage his past?

Furious with himself and the whole damn situation, Christian turned to go, but stopped when Trevor spoke up again.

"What's eating at you, man? You've been terrorizing the staff and *me* for the last couple of days."

Yeah, he had. Wrestling with your demons didn't make for a good time and there were bound to be innocent bystanders caught up in the fight. But Trevor wasn't his enemy and it'd be best to remember that.

Christian looked back at his friend and said, "I've got some things on my mind, that's all."

"Want to talk about it?"

"Not really," he said. He had to get things sorted out

for himself before he could speak to any of the Jarrods about this.

Trevor stared at him, then nodded. "All right. I figure a man's entitled to his secrets. But if you change your mind, I'm here."

"Appreciate it." And he did. He had friends here, Christian knew that. What he didn't have was Erica. "I'll see you later."

Blake walked in the door almost at the same instant and jumped out of the way before Christian could crash right into him. "What's his deal?"

"I don't know. He won't say. Clearly something's bugging him though." Trevor sat down at his desk, ready to dive into the paperwork again.

"I know how he feels," Blake said.

The tone of his voice more than anything else had Trevor looking up. "Why? What's wrong?"

"Not sure. But I just saw Melissa with Shane McDermott. They looked…cozy. Have you heard anything?"

Trevor leaned back in his desk chair. "No. But if our friendly neighborhood rancher is interested in our little sister, I suggest we keep an eye on things."

"Just what I was thinking," Blake agreed.

Three days holed up in her old condo in San Francisco and Erica was no closer to knowing what to do than she had been when she arrived. She'd cried herself silly for the first several hours until her sorrow had faded into fury. Anger was so much easier to deal with.

Erica stood up and moved to the balcony off her

living room. She had a view of the bay and the Golden Gate Bridge and she'd spent most of her days with the sliding glass door open to let in the frigid wind blowing in off the ocean.

After so much time in Colorado, with the sky so wide and open and so much space around her, she felt... caged in the very home she'd once loved so much.

Strange. She'd only been gone three weeks but this place no longer felt like home. She looked at the soft, pastel paintings on the walls and couldn't figure out what she'd seen in them. She wasn't the same woman who had lived here. She'd changed. Grown. She'd reshaped her life to suit the woman she'd become.

Now Erica knew what it was to finally find her place. She had discovered what it was like to love someone and lose. She knew what it was to go on with your heart breaking and not have a clue what to do next.

She'd found more than a home in Colorado.

She'd found herself. And the woman she was today needed answers to questions she was no longer afraid to ask. She hadn't run from Christian; she'd run *toward* her past. After leaving him at the river, Erica had realized that she couldn't enjoy a future without first dealing with her past. And so she'd come back to San Francisco. To tie up the loose ends of her life so that she could return to the place she belonged.

Okay, yes, she hadn't immediately gone to face her father. But she was going to. She'd simply needed a few days to sort out her own feelings. That didn't mean she was turning tail and running. And she certainly wasn't going to hide here in a condo that wasn't really *hers* anymore.

She was going back.

Just as soon as she found what she needed to know.

Ten

The very next morning Erica marched into her father's office and faced him, for the first time not as his daughter, but as an adult who demanded respect.

"Erica," Walter said, standing up and moving out from behind his desk. "You didn't tell me you were coming."

"No." She studied his familiar features and saw with surprise that he looked older than she remembered. And not as intimidating, either. Was it her imagination? she wondered. Or was it that she was no longer looking at him as a child would?

"Are you all right?" He came to her, gave her a brief, awkward hug, then stepped back.

The embrace was over so quickly it was almost as if

it hadn't happened at all. Erica felt the sting of tears in her eyes and inwardly groaned. She fought to hold those tears at bay as she asked, "I need to know something, Father, and I need the truth."

"Of course."

"Did you ever love me?"

"What kind of question is that?" His eyes narrowed and his scowl deepened. "Is this what they've been telling you in Colorado? Those Jarrods have been filling your head with nonsense and you've been listening?"

Shaking her head, Erica felt her heart sink. "They haven't said a word about you, Father. This is something I need to know. Did you love me? Ever?"

His mouth tightened into a straight, grim line as if he were deliberately holding back the words she needed to hear.

Walking past him, she dropped her cream-colored leather bag onto the nearest chair, then turned to face him again. "I'm tired, Father. And hurt. And a little miserable, too. I'm finally figuring out who I am, but to finish doing that, I have to know who I was. Was I *ever* a daughter to you?"

As if all the air had left his body suddenly, Walter Prentice seemed to shrink in size right before her eyes. His shoulders slumped, his head dipped until his chin met his chest. Tiredly he lifted both hands to rub his face, then dropped them again and looked up at her.

She walked toward him, drawn by the naked pain on his face. Erica had never seen this side of her father.

Never known him to be emotional at all. She took a shallow breath and held it.

"You're more like your mother than you know, Erica. You have her beauty, but more important, you have her heart." Leaning forward, he took her hands in his and held them gently. "I do love you, child. Always have. I couldn't love you more if you were my own blood."

A great weight eased off her heart and Erica took her first easy breath since walking into his office. "Then why? Why have you always kept me at a distance? Why would you never let me get close? You wouldn't even let me work here, Father. I thought you believed I wasn't good enough to join the family business."

"Ah, God, I've made so many mistakes," he muttered, his grip on her hands tightening. "But I swear they were made with the best of intentions. For years I was afraid that Don would try to take you from me, so I tried to keep an emotional distance from you. Fearing that if I did lose you, the pain would be too great to bear." He sighed heavily. "Then the years passed and I kept you tucked away, out of the family business, to protect you from Don Jarrod."

"What? That makes no sense."

"It did to me. I was terrified that he'd come back, you see. Try to take you from me as he stole your mother. I couldn't bear the thought of that."

"Oh, Dad…"

He squeezed her hands. "Do you realize that's the first time you've ever called me that? To you, I was always 'Father,' not 'Dad.'"

Erica sighed and let go of the pain and misery she'd been carrying around for most of her life. Sad as it was, it was also sort of comforting to know that neither one of them had deliberately shunned the other. Mistakes had been made, true, but by both of them and for far too long.

Leaning into his warm embrace, she wrapped her arms around her father's neck and let the tears flow. He patted her gently and whispered words of comfort that were too soft for her ears to catch—but her heart heard and slowly began to heal.

"Are you happy out there?"

Erica sat across from her father and smiled. It was the first time she could ever remember her father being concerned with her happiness. But then, there had been a lot of firsts today. She felt lighter, freer than she had in years. She'd accomplished so much in just leaving, taking her own life in her hands. She'd found who she was meant to be. She'd reconnected with the father who had loved and raised her. And she had found—and lost—Christian.

Her smile faded, but she forced it back into place. "I really am. I know it's strange. I can hardly believe it myself, to tell you the truth. But it's so gorgeous there, Dad." Funny how easily that name spilled from her now that she knew her affection was welcome. "I don't just mean the resort, but Colorado itself. It's huge and open and so beautiful it's almost hard to look at it. I hope one day you'll come to visit me there."

Clearly uncomfortable at the thought, he was quiet for a moment, his brow furrowed and his eyes narrowed. "I'll come. Don Jarrod's ghost won't keep me away from my daughter, Erica. I'm not going to risk losing you again."

Her heart opened even further as love swept in, chasing away years of regrets and misery. "You won't lose me, Dad. You can't. I love you."

He reached across the table and took her hand in his for a quick squeeze. "Does my heart good to hear that, I don't mind telling you. But the most important thing is you're happy, right?"

"I was...." How to explain to him what a mess she'd made of everything? She couldn't actually confess to her father that she'd seduced a man who didn't want her, after all.

"What changed?"

She folded her linen napkin and set it on the table. Then sitting back in her chair, she said, "I fell in love."

"And this makes you miserable?"

"No," she said on a short laugh, "it made me happier than I've ever been before."

"But..." Walter encouraged her to talk just by patiently waiting.

Smiling, she acknowledged, "You've still got the intimidation knack."

"It's a gift," he said with a wink. "Now, tell me what's wrong with this man that he doesn't see what a wonderful girl you are."

"There's nothing wrong with him," she said, Christian's face rising up in her mind to taunt her. "He just doesn't want me enough."

"Well, why the hell not?"

"It's complicated, Dad. I think he does care for me. But he won't let himself." Irritation spiked inside her and she had to take a deep breath just to calm herself. "So the question is, how am I supposed to live there and see him every day feeling the way I do?"

"What's the alternative?" he asked briskly. "Run away? Hide? Pretend you don't feel what you do?"

"I don't know," she whispered.

"Well, I do," Walter said, standing to come around the table. He pulled her from her chair and stood her up in front of him. With the tips of his fingers, he tilted her chin up until she was looking directly into his eyes. "You're a Prentice, Erica. And we don't run. We don't put our heads in the sand when things don't go our way, either. If you love that dolt, then find a way to make him admit he loves you, too."

Throwing her arms around his neck, she hugged him tightly and sighed when Walter's arms came around her with a fierce embrace.

"I love you, Dad," she whispered and his embrace tightened in response.

"I love you, too, little girl," he whispered. "Guess you'll be leaving right away?"

She pulled back and smiled up at him. "I really should. The gala opens next week and there are a million details to see to—not to mention the fact that there's a certain man I have to see and talk to."

"Do I get to know his name?"

"As soon as I straighten him out, I'll introduce you," she promised, then gave him an extra hug for good measure. Grabbing up her purse, she raced for the door, but stopped dead when her father called out her name.

"Yes?"

He wagged a finger at her. "Just don't you forget who you are, little girl. You're Erica Prentice. *My* daughter. And you can do anything you put your mind to."

She grinned at him. "You're damn right I can."

Christian refused to live like this any longer. He hadn't seen or spoken to Erica in days. For all he knew, she could have decided to forego her inheritance and move back to San Francisco. That thought drove spikes through his mind and heart. What if she didn't return? What if she decided that staying at Jarrod Ridge would be too painful because *he* was an idiot?

His stomach felt like a ball of lead had settled in it, while at the same time, his chest felt hollowed out. He scrubbed both hands across his face and stood up. Turning, he faced the window and didn't even see the spectacular view. Instead, he saw Erica as she'd been their last night together by the river.

Naked, open, holding her arms out to him, taking him into her body, her heart. He could see the warmth in her eyes and the soft smile wreathing her face. His insides twisted and his mouth dried up. He loved her.

He loved Erica Prentice.

And he'd not only let her walk away, he'd been ass enough to ruin what had been the best damn night of his life. The question now was, was he going to let that mistake stand? Or was he going to do everything in his power to correct it?

"Screw this," he said out loud to no one. He turned and looked around the interior of his office. The one he'd worked so hard for—and all he saw was emptiness. In his mind, his future stretched out in front of him and that, too, was empty.

Pointless.

What the hell good was the job of his dreams if the woman he needed wasn't a part of his life?

Furious with himself for taking this long to realize what was the most important thing to him, Christian jumped up from the desk chair and marched out of the room. He needed to talk to the oldest Jarrod sibling and he knew exactly where to find him.

Twenty minutes later, he was searching for Blake Jarrod amid the throng of people wandering around the site for the gala. The man was out here somewhere directing the crews setting up. When he spotted him, Christian headed right at him.

"Christian," the other man said with a nod of greeting. "What are you doing out here? Giving up law to come swing a hammer with us?"

"No," he said, barely glancing at the crew. "Blake, I need to talk to you."

"Sure," he said, heading to a less crowded part of the lawn. He stopped and crossed his arms over his chest. "What's this about, Christian?"

The only way to handle this was to jump right in.

"I'm resigning as family attorney as of today," Christian said and felt a weight slide off his shoulders. Damn, it felt good to be a free man. He'd been living an indentured life and he hadn't even realized it until just this instant.

All along, he had thought he was steering his own course. Plotting his own life and destiny. But in reality, Don Jarrod had still been in charge. Even from the grave. But not anymore. And never again.

"What?" Astonished, Blake reached out, grabbed Christian's upper arm and dragged him a little farther away to make sure no one would overhear them. "You can't resign. Are you nuts?"

"Not anymore," he said, grinning. "And yeah, I can resign. Watch me."

"We can't run this place without you, Christian!"

"Not my problem as of today, Blake. Sorry, but this is how it has to be."

"Sorry?" Blake threw his hands high and let them slap down against his thighs. "You're *sorry* that you're walking out just as we all get back and have to deal with mountains of crap?"

"You've got each other. You'll do fine. This is your home, Blake."

"It's your home as much as it is ours."

Christian looked around, letting his gaze scan the familiar grounds, the guests and the well-trained staff. True, this was his home. But it didn't mean a damn to him without Erica. Decision made, he turned back to Blake.

"I'll type up a formal letter and leave it with your assistant," he said. "If you want, I can make some recommendations about who I think would work well here."

"I don't want your recommendations," Blake muttered with a dark frown. "I want you here, doing your job. Like always."

"Can't do it, Blake," Christian said. He wasn't thinking about Blake. He was thinking about Erica. He had to tell Erica he loved her and that he was willing to risk everything in his life *except* her.

"You have to do it. We can't afford to lose you." Blake took a deep breath, bit back his frustration and demanded, "You've always been happy here, Christian. Where's this coming from?"

"Things are different now."

"Since when?" Blake's eyes narrowed on him.

He hadn't intended to say anything. But how could he not? Blake was a friend and the brother of the woman he loved. Why the hell should he hide his feelings now? He took a breath and plunged in.

"Since your sister."

"Melissa?"

"No." Christian laughed out loud at the stunned

surprise on Blake's face. Clearly he'd done a very good job of keeping his feelings to himself. "Erica."

"Really?" Blake shook his head. "Huh. I didn't have a clue."

"Nobody does," Christian told him. "That's the point. I've been hiding how I feel about her because of my responsibilities here."

"What?" Now Blake just looked confused. "Why would you do that?"

Christian sighed. "You know as well as I do how your father felt about what he called 'fraternizing.'"

"Oh, for God's sake—"

Christian kept going. "I get involved with your sister, I lose my position here and any shares I have in the company. The board of directors will take care of that at their next meeting."

"So you're just gonna walk away from everything you've ever known instead."

"Rather than lose her? Yeah. In a heartbeat."

Blake nodded and grinned at him. "I can see that. What you didn't think about is, the Jarrod family won't let you resign."

"You can't stop me."

"No, but I can hire you again the minute you quit," Blake told him. "And when I do, there'll be no restrictions, Christian."

"What are you saying?"

"I'm saying what everybody knows. Don Jarrod was a hard man. I'm not him. And neither are my brothers." Blake laughed aloud. "God, Christian, Melissa would kill us all if we let you leave over something like this."

Christian shook his head as if he couldn't believe how this conversation was going. He'd been prepared to lose everything to keep Erica. Now it seemed he was going to have it all. If he could convince the woman he loved that he deserved her.

Slapping him on the shoulder, Blake said, "We'll write up a new contract between you and the Jarrod Resort whenever you're ready."

"I don't know what to say."

"I think that's a first," Blake told him with a laugh. "So you and Erica, huh?" His eyes went cool and serious for a moment. "I've had my issues with the new sister, but bottom line here is, she *is* my sister. So just to put you on alert—if you're not actually planning to marry her—you won't have a job to worry about. None of us will stand by and let anybody hurt her."

"I don't want to hurt her. I want to marry her. All I have to do is convince her to say yes."

"Good luck, man." Blake held out a hand toward him. "And welcome to the family."

Christian shook his friend's hand and hoped to hell his talk with Erica would go as well.

By the time the Jarrod jet landed at the small strip in Aspen, Erica was a woman on a mission. She was focused. Determined. She had her plan on facing down Christian all worked out and was eager to get on with it.

But her lovely, well-thought-out plan dissolved as she disembarked from the plane and saw a car waiting for her. The driver, an older man with grizzled black-and-white hair, smiled as he held out an envelope.

Curious, Erica opened it while the driver stacked her luggage in the trunk of the car. The note inside was short and in Melissa's handwriting. *Get in the car and don't ask any questions.*

A spurt of irritation briefly shot through Erica, because now she'd have to wait to take care of the most important confrontation in her life. But just as quickly, she let go of her disappointment and told herself that her conversation with a hardheaded man could wait a while longer. If Melissa had gone to this much trouble, she must need Erica for something.

"Okay, then," she said, smiling at her driver, "guess we should get going."

"Yes, ma'am." He opened the car door, saw her settled, then climbed behind the wheel. In a few minutes they were on the road to the resort and Erica was wondering what Melissa was up to. She had called her sister to let her know that she was coming home, so if there had been something wrong, wouldn't Melissa have told her about it already?

Home.

That word settled in her heart and she had to smile. Oddly enough, after only three short weeks at Jarrod Ridge, the place *had* become home to Erica. She wasn't the same person she'd been when she arrived. Now, she was officially an *ex* big-city girl. She'd officially quit her job. Oh, she'd have to go back to San Francisco soon, to arrange for the sale of her condo and to have her furniture shipped west. But she'd take care of that and get back to Jarrod Ridge as quickly as possible.

This was where she belonged now.

Her gaze scanned the scenery as it passed in a green-brown blur, her mind racing, dragging up image after image of Christian. She worried over how their talk would go and told herself that no matter what else happened, she would at least have the satisfaction of knowing she'd told him how she felt. If he still chose to walk away from her—well, she'd just make his life a living hell until he changed his mind.

In no time at all, the car was pulling through the resort's front gate. But instead of heading toward the hotel entry, the driver drove off on what had to be a service road. She looked behind her as the Manor receded into the distance and was then swallowed up by the cloud of dust flying up from behind the wheels of the car.

"Just where are we going?" she asked, despite Melissa's note.

"Only a minute or two more, miss," the man said.

The trees were thicker here, lining either side of the road like soldiers at parade rest. She didn't recognize this area and realized that there was still a lot of the resort for her to explore and come to know. But she hadn't planned on doing it right now.

Finally the car came to a stop on the rutted road. The

driver helped her out, pointed to the tree line on her left and said, "Just head right through there, miss."

Before she could ask any questions, the driver had hopped back into the car and disappeared down the road. "Perfect. What is going on?"

She headed off to her left and cocked her head to listen when she heard a familiar roar of sound. It was the river. Her heart started pounding and a tiny curl of nerves unspooled in the pit of her stomach. Still, she walked on, until she rounded a bend and saw a blanket spread out under the trees. Her breath caught in her chest as she realized that the driver had brought her to Christian's spot alongside the river. Since they'd taken the back way in, she hadn't recognized the place until now.

On that blanket was a silver ice bucket holding what looked like a bottle of champagne, and a picnic basket, its lid partially opened to allow a baguette to spear up.

Erica took a deep breath and when Christian stepped out from behind a tree, she felt hope and confusion tangle inside her. When she could speak without her voice breaking, she asked, "What's this about, Christian?"

"I needed to talk to you and I thought the best place to do that was here. In our spot."

Our spot. Not his. *Ours.* That brief flash of hope she'd experienced began to shine more brightly. But even as it did, she wondered if maybe he'd brought her here to tell her he'd never love her. Maybe he had chosen this particular spot to soften the blow of goodbye. So before he could speak, she did. "I have a few things I want to say to you, too."

He came toward her, stepping out of the dappled shade into the wash of golden sunlight. "First hear me out, Erica."

"No." She skipped back out of reach of him, because she knew if he touched her, the words would dry up in her mind and she'd forget everything but the feeling of having his hands on her again. "Let me say this. I've been rehearsing it all the way here and I need to get it out."

"Okay, then. Tell me."

Nodding, she pointed at the picnic he'd set up in the shade and said, "First, let me say if you've brought me here to tell me goodbye, you can forget it."

"Goodbye?" Christian reached for her, but she moved back and away again, frustrating him beyond belief. "I'm not—"

"Because I'm not going anywhere," she said, lifting her chin and glaring at him. "I'm going to be right here. Every day. You'll have to see me, work with me, talk with me. Every day. And every day I'm going to remind you of how good we are together. Of what we could have had together if only you'd made the right choice. And I'm going to keep on reminding you of that until I convince you that we should be together even if it takes me another twenty years."

Tears were shining in her eyes and that alone tore at Christian's heart and soul. "Don't, Erica. Don't cry."

"I'm not crying," she argued. "I'm arguing, and arguing makes me emotional."

"I can see that," he said, smiling now because she still loved him. Still wanted him. He hadn't ruined everything after all. "Now, will you listen to me?"

She sniffed, cast a look at the champagne picnic, then turned back to him. "I suppose."

"Good, because you're not going to have to remind me for twenty years. Not even for twenty minutes."

"I'm not?"

He walked to her, closing the distance between them with three long steps. He looked down into her whiskey-colored eyes and saw everything he had ever wanted shining back at him. How could he have thought for even one minute that he would be willing to do without her? That he would be *able* to be without her?

Not a chance.

"I went to Blake while you were gone and I quit my job as family attorney."

"What?" She pushed at him. "You can't do that! I won't let you give up everything you worked for just because Don Jarrod was a medieval warlord. And Blake shouldn't allow it, I'm going to—"

Christian laughed as she turned from teary to warrior in the blink of an eye. God, life with her was going to be fascinating. "You don't have to do anything. Blake refused to let me resign. Said he'd just hire me again without all the qualifiers his father insisted on."

"So you're not leaving?"

"No."

She watched him warily. "And you're not going to pull away from me again?"

"No." He pulled her into his arms and held her tightly to him until he felt her return his embrace, her arms winding about his waist as she clung to him. Then his world righted and Christian knew everything was going to be all right. "I'm never letting you go again. I love you, Erica. Have from the moment I met you. When you left..."

He pulled back and stared down into her eyes. He lifted one hand to cup her cheek and then smoothed his fingers through her hair, loving the cool, slick slide of it against his skin. "When you left, you took my heart with you. I knew then that nothing I had, nothing I had worked for, was worth anything without you in my life."

She sighed, and a soft, amazingly beautiful smile curved her mouth as she looked up at him. "Christian, I love you so much."

"Thank God," he muttered.

She laughed a little. "I thought for sure I'd have to argue for hours to convince you that you loved me."

"No arguments necessary," he said. Then he reached into his pocket, pulled out a small, dark red velvet box and opening it, held it out to her.

Sunlight danced off the enormous diamond and shone in her eyes as he watched her. He took the ring from the box and slid it onto her finger, all while she simply stared up at him, with a bemused smiled on her lovely face.

"I finally figured it out."

"What?" she asked, glancing down at the beautiful promise glittering on her hand.

"That all I need is you. If I have you, I have everything. Without you, there's nothing."

"Oh, Christian…" Tears fell, sliding along her cheeks, but her smile was as brilliant as the diamond on her finger.

"Marry me, Erica. Make a family with me."

"Yes!" she shouted the single word, then laughed in delight. "Yes, I'll marry you and I swear, I will love you forever."

He kissed her hard and fast, then drew back and grinned at her. Erica threw her arms around his neck and hung on for all she was worth as he swung her into a dizzying circle. The world rushed by, a blur of color and sound, but in the center of it all, they were together.

As they were meant to be.

* * * * *

Don't miss Guy Jarrod's sexy story,
FALLING FOR HIS PROPER MISTRESS,
part of the DYNASTIES: THE JARRODS
from Silhouette Desire.

COMING NEXT MONTH

Available August 10, 2010

#2029 HONOR-BOUND GROOM
Yvonne Lindsay
Man of the Month

#2030 FALLING FOR HIS PROPER MISTRESS
Tessa Radley
Dynasties: The Jarrods

#2031 WINNING IT ALL
"Pregnant with the Playboy's Baby"—Catherine Mann
"His Accidental Fiancée"—Emily McKay
A Summer for Scandal

#2032 EXPECTANT PRINCESS, UNEXPECTED AFFAIR
Michelle Celmer
Royal Seductions

#2033 THE BILLIONAIRE'S BABY ARRANGEMENT
Charlene Sands
Napa Valley Vows

#2034 HIS BLACK SHEEP BRIDE
Anna DePalo

SDCNM0710

REQUEST YOUR FREE BOOKS!

2 FREE NOVELS PLUS 2 FREE GIFTS!

Passionate, Powerful, Provocative!

YES! Please send me 2 FREE Silhouette Desire® novels and my 2 FREE gifts (gifts are worth about $10). After receiving them, if I don't wish to receive any more books, I can return the shipping statement marked "cancel." If I don't cancel, I will receive 6 brand-new novels every month and be billed just $4.05 per book in the U.S. or $4.74 per book in Canada. That's a saving of at least 15% off the cover price! It's quite a bargain! Shipping and handling is just 50¢ per book.* I understand that accepting the 2 free books and gifts places me under no obligation to buy anything. I can always return a shipment and cancel at any time. Even if I never buy another book, the two free books and gifts are mine to keep forever.

225/326 SDN E5QG

Name _____ (PLEASE PRINT)

Address _____ Apt. #

City _____ State/Prov. _____ Zip/Postal Code

Signature (if under 18, a parent or guardian must sign)

Mail to the Silhouette Reader Service:

IN U.S.A.: P.O. Box 1867, Buffalo, NY 14240-1867
IN CANADA: P.O. Box 609, Fort Erie, Ontario L2A 5X3

Not valid for current subscribers to Silhouette Desire books.

Want to try two free books from another line?
Call 1-800-873-8635 or visit www.morefreebooks.com.

* Terms and prices subject to change without notice. Prices do not include applicable taxes. N.Y. residents add applicable sales tax. Canadian residents will be charged applicable provincial taxes and GST. Offer not valid in Quebec. This offer is limited to one order per household. All orders subject to approval. Credit or debit balances in a customer's account(s) may be offset by any other outstanding balance owed by or to the customer. Please allow 4 to 6 weeks for delivery. Offer available while quantities last.

Your Privacy: Silhouette Books is committed to protecting your privacy. Our Privacy Policy is available online at www.eHarlequin.com or upon request from the Reader Service. From time to time we make our lists of customers available to reputable third parties who may have a product or service of interest to you. If you would prefer we not share your name and address, please check here. ☐

Help us get it right—We strive for accurate, respectful and relevant communications. To clarify or modify your communication preferences, visit us at www.ReaderService.com/consumerschoice.

SDES10R

HARLEQUIN®

A Romance

FOR EVERY MOOD™

Spotlight on

— Heart & Home —

Heartwarming romances
where love can happen
right when you least expect it.

See the next page to enjoy a sneak peek
from Harlequin® American Romance®,
a Heart and Home series.

Five hunky Texas single fathers—five stories from Cathy Gillen Thacker's LONE STAR DADS *miniseries. Here's an excerpt from the latest,* THE MOMMY PROPOSAL *from Harlequin American Romance.*

"I hear you work miracles," Nate Hutchinson drawled. Brooke Mitchell had just stepped into his lavishly appointed office in downtown Fort Worth, Texas.

"Sometimes, I do." Brooke smiled and took the sexy financier's hand in hers, shook it briefly.

"Good." Nate looked her straight in the eye. "Because I'm in need of a home makeover—fast. The son of an old friend is coming to live with me."

She was still tingling from the feel of his warm palm. "Temporarily or permanently?"

"If all goes according to plan, I'll adopt Landry by summer's end."

Brooke had heard the founder of Nate Hutchinson Financial Services was eligible, wealthy and generous to a fault. She hadn't known he was in the market for a family, but she supposed she shouldn't be surprised. But Brooke had figured a man as successful and handsome as Nate would want one the old-fashioned way. *Not that this was any of her business...*

"So what's the child like?" she asked crisply, trying not to think how the marine-blue of Nate's dress shirt deepened the hue of his eyes.

"I don't know." Nate took a seat behind his massive antique mahogany desk. He relaxed against the smooth leather of the chair. "I've never met him."

"Yet you've invited this kid to live with you permanently?"

"It's complicated. But I'm sure it's going to be fine."

Obviously Nate Hutchinson knew as little about teenage

boys as he did about decorating. But that wasn't her problem. Finding a way to do the assignment without getting the least bit emotionally involved was.

Find out how a young boy brings Nate and Brooke together in THE MOMMY PROPOSAL, coming August 2010 from Harlequin American Romance.

THE HEAT IS ON

by

Jill Shalvis

The attraction between Bella and
Detective Madden is undeniable.
But can a few wild encounters
turn into love?

Don't miss this hot read.

*Available in August
where books are sold.*

red-hot reads

HB79562

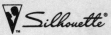

HARLEQUIN
Ambassadors

Want to share your passion for reading Harlequin® Books?

Become a Harlequin Ambassador!

Harlequin Ambassadors are a group of passionate and well-connected readers who are willing to share their joy of reading Harlequin® books with family and friends.

You'll be sent all the tools you need to spark great conversation, including free books!

All we ask is that you share the romance with your friends and family!

You'll also be invited to have a say in new book ideas and exchange opinions with women just like you!

To see if you qualify* to be a Harlequin Ambassador, please visit **www.HarlequinAmbassadors.com.**

*Please note that not everyone who applies to be a Harlequin Ambassador will qualify. For more information please visit www.HarlequinAmbassadors.com.

Thank you for your participation.